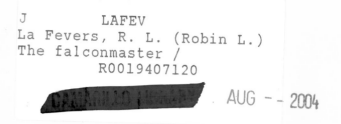

The
Falconmaster

The Falconmaster

R. L. La Fevers

DUTTON CHILDREN'S BOOKS

NEW YORK

CIP Data is available.

Published in the United States 2003 by Dutton Children's Books,
a division of Penguin Young Readers Group
345 Hudson Street, New York, New York 10014
www.penguin.com

Printed in USA • Designed by Tim Hall
ISBN 0-525-46993-1
First Edition
1 3 5 7 9 10 8 6 4 2

To my father,

Arthur Clarke,

whose never-ending belief in me

has been a wonderful foundation

on which to build my dreams

The
Falconmaster

chapter · 1 ·

WAT PEERED AROUND THE CORNER WITH HIS ONE GOOD eye.

"I'd be careful if I was you." A thin, rasping voice startled him, and he jerked back from the doorway.

"If they catch you, they'll make you sorry," the voice continued.

Wat turned toward the stone wall and spotted tiny John Thatcher huddled in the dark shadows. "Maybe," he agreed. "But they'll have to catch me first."

The small boy snorted. "Like that would be hard, catching a cripple."

Wat flushed angrily.

The boy continued. "They'll cut off your hand or put out your eye or somefin'."

The lad knew better than most. The whole village had watched as his father was hung from the gibbet for poaching in his lordship's forest. They left his body to hang, a grisly warning to all who had once hunted in the nearby forests that were now forbidden to them. His youngest son had taken to begging outside the manor kitchens ever since. Wat had nearly stumbled over the scrawny lad many times as he made his own risky trips to the kitchen to sneak some food.

"Well, I won't make the mistake of taking something big, like your da. I'll take something small they won't miss."

The boy shrugged as if it made no difference to him. "It's your scrawny neck they'll hang. Not mine."

Ignoring the boy, Wat turned back to the delicious smells pouring out of the manor kitchen. He clutched his hand to his middle, trying to soften the gnawing hunger. If he didn't get something to eat soon, he was afraid he would begin gnawing the dirt clods that littered the courtyard. Ever since the Normans had come, hunger was a constant companion. The harsh conquerors had harrowed the land, putting torch to the fields and farms, laying the ground waste so no rebellion could grow. Wat had been hungry for two years now.

Wat leaned farther forward, trying to judge Cook's mood. If he was in a pleasant frame of mind, things could go well and his mother might slip him some scraps. If Cook was in a fitful state, then everyone would be foul-tempered. All Wat could expect then was a whack across his shoulders with a broom. That and more gnawing hunger until nightfall, when his mother would try again to sneak him a bit of something.

Wat had learned two lessons in his ten summers. One was that dung rolled downhill. The second was that it usually managed to find him rather quickly.

The sound of clanging pots, sizzling fat, and shrill voices mixed among gruff commands assaulted Wat's ears. The frantic activity did not bode well.

Cook stood by the hearth, sweat pouring down his beefy, reddened face. He picked up the huge meat hook, which leaned close to the fire.

"Blood of the Saints!" he bellowed, dropping the hook. Turning to Ralph the spit-turner, he thwacked him upside the head. "How many times have I told you not to leave that handle so close to the fire?"

Still staggering from the blow, Ralph tried to defend himself. "But I never even touched—"

"Get out of my way, you thickheaded turnip!"

Looking sullen, Ralph scuttled back to a safe distance. Cook hastily wrapped his burned hand with a thick piece of cloth and picked up the meat hook again. The entire kitchen staff held their breath as he approached the hearth. Grunting with the effort, he reached out and sank the end of the hook into the roast pig and removed it from the spit.

He carried the heavy meat across the room and laid it on the waiting platter. Everyone let out a sigh of relief and returned to their duties. Nothing ruined Cook's day worse than dropping his fine dinner on the floor. Wat never quite understood this. He would gladly eat a roast pig even if it had been dropped on the floor and rolled for ten paces. But then, Cook was a picky fellow. All the Normans were.

Filling their arms with platters, trays, and pitchers, the servers left the kitchen and headed for the connecting door to the great hall, where Lord Sherborne and his guests awaited their meal. As soon as the room was empty, Cook disappeared through a small door at the far end of the kitchen that led to the buttery. According to Wat's mother, the man often grabbed a quick tankard of ale as his just reward for preparing another successful meal.

When Wat was certain he could hear nothing but the crackle of the fire and distant sounds from the great hall, he crept to one of the platters left sitting on the table. It held a tantalizing assortment of meat pies that smelled so good, Wat feared he would drool over the lot of them. Licking his lips, he studied them carefully, wanting to choose only the plumpest, fattest one.

"Hey you! Get away from those pies!"

Wat snatched his hand back and looked up to see Ralph

the spit-turner standing in the doorway, the imprint of Cook's hand still red on his face.

"Get out!" The boy's voice was filled with outrage. "We don't feed devil's spawn around here!" Ralph strode over to the hearth and grabbed the meat hook. His eyes narrowed, and an unpleasant smile appeared on his big ugly face. "I'll teach you to hang about the kitchen door."

The dung was starting to roll downhill.

Wat turned and bolted. He ran out through the kitchen doorway and stumbled into the courtyard. He tried to gather some speed but was hampered by his useless left leg as it dragged behind him. He fought the urge to turn and see how close behind Ralph was. Stopping to look would slow him down, and he didn't dare risk it, even when he heard a loud "oomph" and a clatter as something hit the ground.

Ralph's voice rang out. "Watch out, you little goat turd!"

"I was just sitting here . . ."

Tiny John Thatcher's words were lost as Wat moved out of hearing range. He passed into the outer courtyard, his feet slapping out an uneven rhythm on the rough stones. The sound of his own breathing filled his ears, and he couldn't be certain how close Ralph was behind him.

Dodging chickens and pigs, and a villager or two, Wat kept to the shadows of the walls as much as he could, trying to make his way to the outer bailey. A cold, bitter fear settled into the pit of his stomach as he heard the voices of other village boys join Ralph's. There were few things they considered as fine a sport as chasing a half-blind cripple. Since most of the villagers were convinced he was begotten by the devil—why else would he be blind in one eye and have such a misshapen foot?—he knew that no one would lift a finger to help him.

He also knew that sometimes he could get away, and sometimes he couldn't. Partly running, mostly sliding, Wat made his way down the steep drawbridge that led toward the outer bailey.

The voices drew closer. With this many in on the chase, Wat knew there was a good chance they would catch him. He fought back a wave of panic, reminding himself that he had survived their beatings in the past. But then, they'd never been carrying a meat hook before.

Skidding around the corner by the smith's yard, Wat startled a group of pigeons that had been hiding under the water trough. He hadn't seen them at first, not until their flapping wings caught his attention. Desperate now, the voices right behind him, he checked his stride and turned toward the trough. He was out of time. He could only hope that if the trough had hidden the pigeons that well, then maybe it would work for him.

His breath came in ragged, tearing gasps as he hunkered down and crawled into the small space. His hands and knees settled into the pigeon feathers and droppings that covered the ground, but he ignored them. Droppings were nothing compared with flying fists and kicking feet, to say nothing of the meat hook.

Wat drew himself down as small as possible and cleared his mind of all thoughts. As his breathing eased, he tried to imagine he was nothing but a plump, gray pigeon. He pictured himself covered in soft, gray feathers, hiding from predators by staying still under the brush. Trying to calm his heart, which hammered painfully in his chest, he filled his mind with the sound of cooing.

All too soon, he heard the sound of running feet and loud voices come tearing around the corner. He ignored the excited shouts and yells that almost sounded like gibberish in his ears, and concentrated on being small and invisible.

Without so much as a pause, the footsteps went past him. A little farther on he heard their footsteps slow down and their voices raised in confusion and frustration.

"Where did he get to this time?"

"I know I saw him come 'round the corner."

A loud, booming voice interrupted their puzzled questions. "Get on now! All of you! I don't want your kind of trouble around here!"

Wat recognized the voice of Olin, the blacksmith, and let out a deep sigh of relief. All of the village lads respected his large, heavily muscled arms and brawny strength. Since he had a temper to match, no one ever dared argue with him. Wat heard Ralph's voice mumble something about meaning no harm.

"Go!" Olin bellowed so loudly that it caused the water trough Wat hid under to shudder. The boys lowered their voices, and Wat listened to the sound of their footsteps as they went off in different directions.

He had hardly taken a deep breath of relief before a huge arm, blackened with soot, reached in and grabbed him by the shoulder.

"And I don't want you skulking around my smith, either!"

Yanked to a standing position, Wat found himself face-to-face with Olin, whose coarse features glistened under a fine layer of sweat. The blacksmith held a hammer the length of a man's leg in his left hand as easily as if it were a twig.

"I don't care how thick that head of yours is, boy, when

it comes up against an iron poker, it's going to burst like an overripe plum. Now stay away from those lads. Stay away from here, too." The blacksmith let go of Wat and gave him a little shove. "I don't know why they didn't see you there," he muttered. "You were hiding in plain sight."

Olin looked away from Wat, then froze. Slowly, Wat turned around and saw his mother standing behind him, all the color drained from her face.

"An iron poker?" she asked, her voice wobbling.

Wat sickened when he realized his mother had overheard. He worked hard to keep the realities of the villagers' torment from her, knowing it wounded her more than him.

"Brenna . . ." Olin's voice softened as he spoke the name. "What are you doing here?"

Wat's mother took two steps forward, then stopped. "I heard shouts and yelling, and the word 'cripple.' I thought Wat was in trouble."

"Well, he was," Olin said matter-of-factly. "And now he's out of it." Olin glanced over at Wat, and a look of true understanding passed between them. Wat's mother need not know. "He's a big lad now, Brenna. He can take care of himself."

Olin put his hand on her elbow to gently steer her away, but she jerked from his hold and came to stand in front of

Wat. Her eyes nearly burned holes in his skin as she searched for the truth.

"Are you truly all right? Did they . . ." Her voice faded. She couldn't bring herself to give voice to the words.

"Truly, I am fine, Mother," Wat said.

Olin stepped forward again, and this time she let him take her elbow. "Come now, we must get you back to the kitchen before they notice you're gone. You've already got one mark against you." He nodded his head in Wat's direction. "You don't want to be handing them excuses on a platter, now, do you?"

Brenna shook her head and let Olin escort her to the edge of the smith yard, where he gently nudged her toward the manor. She looked over her shoulder one more time at Wat. He gave her a cheerful smile, and some of the tenseness left her face.

As soon as she'd left, Olin hurried back to Wat. "Go on, now," Olin said, his voice gruff. "Stay out of trouble so you don't break your ma's heart."

"Aye," Wat said, wondering when Olin had come to care so much about his mother's heart.

Wat turned to leave the yard, then glanced back over his shoulder to study his hiding spot. Now that he looked, he had to agree it didn't offer much cover. Maybe he had been lucky. His mother always said he was born under fortune's star, but he wasn't convinced. Days like today laid challenge to her claim.

Enough. There was no point in staying here any longer. It was time to move on. He began to make his way through the village to the castle gate.

When he reached the gatehouse, he squared his shoulders and lifted his head high, doing his best to stand up as straight and tall as possible. As he limped through the gate and down the drawbridge, the sentry on duty kept his eyes focused straight ahead, but his fingers fluttered together as he formed the sign to ward off evil.

chapter

· 2 ·

WAT CROSSED THE DRAWBRIDGE AND STEPPED ONTO THE rough dirt road that led away from the castle. He wove his way past the nearby fields where workers were turning the hay and building it into hillocks. That's where most boys his age spent their time, in the fields, next to their fathers, working the ground, tilling the soil, and bringing in the harvest.

Not having a father left many holes in Wat's life, but this was probably the biggest—not having a place to be, a task to call his own.

He'd been allowed to work in the fields last season, after the village had lost so many men under the crushing fist of Norman rule. It hadn't lasted long before the workers claimed his presence caused everything from trouble among the lads to crop blight and the threat of a poor harvest.

After that, he'd been given other duties—mucking out the stable. Not the good stables that housed the fine horses, but the old shed that sheltered an old nag, two donkeys, and a sow. Castoffs, just like himself.

The fields disappeared and Wat finally reached the orchards, where he allowed himself to let down his guard. No one from the fields or the castle could see him here among the fruit trees.

He ignored his throbbing foot as he wandered among the trees. The soft, warm scent of the ripening fruit was overpowering, and Wat's stomach rumbled in rebellion. All the morning's excitement and his inability to scavenge any breakfast at the manor house had made him painfully hungry. He decided he'd rather die with a full belly than live with this hunger a moment longer. In spite of knowing he was alone, he found himself checking over his shoulder before he reached out and picked two ripe plums from the nearest tree. He bit into the first one and sighed with pleasure as the sweet, sticky juice ran down his chin. He kept walking as he ate, stopping only long enough to toss the two pits off to the side before licking his fingers clean.

As Wat passed through the orchards, the larger, shaggier trees of the forest came into view, calling to him. He could be alone there. Except for an occasional hunting party, few of the villagers ever ventured into the woods. Not since the

Norman lord had declared it as his alone. Every freeman had grown up hunting in that forest, able to fill his belly and those of his family on its bounty. But no longer. Now only his lordship could hunt in the forest, and all the villagers were forbidden. So no matter how hungry they were, they stayed away. Except for the poachers, and Wat, like the rest of the village, did his best to pretend he knew nothing about them.

As Wat stepped under the huge trees, their cool shade settled over him. The very things that kept the other villagers away from the forest were what he liked best about it. The silence, the shadows, the small hunted creatures that lived there. As he wound his way deeper and deeper into the forest, Wat found comfort in the shadows. His shoulders relaxed, and the memory of his close call with Ralph fell away from him like a forgotten cloak. He felt safe and strangely at home amid the silence of the trees. He could think of nothing that lurked in the woods that was as frightening as a foul-tempered Ralph or a bored group of village lads.

Wat slowed his step and moved cautiously as he approached a large clearing where the sun's rays filtered down through a heavy canopy of branches. He had discovered this clearing only a fortnight ago, and just yesterday, while he'd been daydreaming in the grove, he'd spotted two falcons flying high overhead. Their beauty had nearly stolen his breath clean away. He was hoping that if he was cautious and quiet, he might see them again today.

He crept to the base of a huge, ancient oak tree, then, making no sudden moves, lay back and stretched out his tired legs.

His mind wandered away from this morning's near miss, skittering neatly past the temptation of self-pity. His thoughts settled on the billowing white clouds that rode on the breeze high above him. Before long, a small dark shape appeared among all that blue and white. Wat squinted his good eye, trying to see better against the bright light of the sun.

It was one of the falcons! As it swooped and dove, Wat could hardly believe his good fortune. It almost made up for his bleak morning.

Such speed, such skill! His heart soared as he imagined what he could do with those gifts! He would swoop down from high up in the sky and pluck tasty meals from those who had already eaten plenty. He could spy all the village bullies from miles away and be gone before they even knew where he was. If he could fly, it wouldn't matter that one of his feet was useless. If he could see forever with one eye, what need would he have for two? A small, satisfied smile crossed his face and he fell asleep, dreaming of flight.

.   .   .

WHEN WAT AWOKE, THE SHADOWS HAD GROWN, STRETCHing their long skinny limbs across the forest floor. It was cool now; surely that's why he shivered.

He leaped to his feet and began making his way over small rocks and bracken toward the castle. Since there was no one to see, he let himself run, although it was really more of a shuffling trot, and an awkward, uneven one at that.

Not until he placed one foot on the rough wooden planks of the drawbridge did he pause and try to catch his breath. Finally, he straightened and began to cross the bridge, ignoring the trickles of sweat that itched along his spine and under his arms.

It didn't take him long to wind his way through the village to the stables. He kept to the shadows mostly and did his best to ignore the gentle light spilling out of shuttered windows where families huddled together over a stewpot or bit of porridge.

He paused at the doorway to the stable, allowing himself one last sweet-smelling breath of cool night air before he entered. Pig slept fitfully in the straw, snorting and grumbling in his piggish dreams, and the two donkeys wheezed noisily. Pillock, the old nag, whinnied. Wat went over and ran his hand down her bony back, and she turned to nuzzle his hand, easy once she knew it was only him.

Tired after the long gallop back to the fortress, Wat went over to his corner and allowed himself to sink into his own pile of hay. Glad to have finally reached safety, he let out a deep breath and let the day's trials seep from his body.

No sooner had he closed his eyes than he heard the crunch of a step on the gravel outside the stable doorway. His eyes flew open and his heart began pounding like a blacksmith's hammer. Was it Ralph? Had he been waiting all afternoon for him to return?

There was another step, a heavier one this time, followed by a low rumbled whisper: "Brenna."

The first footsteps stilled, and Wat heard his mother whisper back, "Olin? Is that you? What are you doing here?" Relief at his mother's voice poured through his body until he was nearly dizzy with it.

"Checking on you."

"I am fine. You do not need to be here."

"I do need to be here." Wat heard more footsteps, and the

voice drew closer. "Someone needs to watch after you to make sure you don't come to trouble looking after that boy of yours."

"I've told you before, Olin. He's my son, and nothing will change that. He's mine to look after, to see to. And see to him I will."

"I know, I know," the blacksmith growled. There was a long pause, and Wat wondered if Olin had left. When he finally spoke, his voice was soft with longing. "Brenna," he began, "if you'd only let me—"

"Shh," his mother hissed. "We've spoken of this before, and the answer is still no. I can take care of myself and my son. Now go. Please."

The silence stretched out long and tight until Wat finally heard the sound of heavy footsteps moving away from the stables. What had Olin been about to say? If she'd only let him what? As her footsteps reached the stable door, he closed his eyes and settled deeper into the straw, trying to pretend he hadn't overheard.

His mother stepped into the stable and called out, "Wat? Wat, are you awake?"

He stretched and rustled in the straw a bit, to make it seem as if he'd just woken. "Ma? Is that you?"

"Yes," she said, hurrying over and kneeling in the straw

next to him. "Are you all right?" she asked, her voice anxious.

"I'm fine. I spent the day in the forest and got back late, that is all."

"The forest? Is that safe? They might think you're . . ." Her voice drifted off.

"I just sit among the trees and stare up at the sky. So far the Normans haven't made a law against that, have they?"

His mother shook her head in despair. "No, but you need to be more careful than most."

Wat changed the subject. "Why is Olin so interested in how you fared up in the kitchens?" he asked.

She turned from him in the dark shadows, and he could feel the heat of her blush as it ran up her cheeks. "He is trying to be a friend, Wat. That is all."

Deep in his heart, Wat knew she was lying. Blushes weren't for friends.

"Here." His mother changed the subject. "I've brought you some food."

A delicious smell filled the small stable as she pulled something out of the pocket of her tunic—two meat pies.

"Mother! Won't you get in trouble? Won't Cook find out? Or Lord Sherborne?" he asked as he eagerly reached for the pies.

In the dim light Wat could see his mother make a small

face. "His lordship didn't care for them, and now Cook won't touch them and vows never to make them again."

Wat bit into one of the pies, the buttery pastry and savory meat filling as good as anything he'd ever tasted.

"Wat," his mother began, then hesitated.

"What?" he asked around a mouthful of meat pie.

"You'd best stay away from the kitchens for a few days."

Wat looked at his mother and could tell she was holding something back. "Why?"

She squirmed slightly on the scratchy hay. "Ralph is claiming Sherborne refused the pasties because you cursed them."

Wat stopped chewing as the food in his mouth turned to dust. "Cursed them?"

His mother looked down at her hands. "Yes," she whispered.

Wat nearly laughed. If he had the power to curse things, did they really think he'd waste it on a pie? "Mother, you know I didn't curse them."

"I know. But they never believe me where you are concerned."

Wat stared at the half-eaten pie in his hands and wanted to throw it into the stable wall, where he could watch it smash into a thousand pieces.

But he didn't have that luxury. He never knew where the next food was coming from and didn't dare waste any that came his way. Besides, his mother had risked much to bring it to him. He forced himself to take another bite, even though it now tasted like old ashes from the hearth.

"I am so sorry, Wat," his mother began, and he could hear the tears in her voice.

"Don't worry. I will go back into the forest tomorrow and stay there until dark again. I like it there better, anyway." He finished the first pie and carefully put the second one in the pocket of his tunic. He would wait and eat it later, tomorrow perhaps, when hunger once again reminded him he could not afford pride.

chapter

· 3 ·

WAT REACHED HIS FAVORITE CLEARING BY LATE MORNING.
He'd rushed through his chores, anxious to be well on the
way to the forest while everyone else was still busy getting
ready for the day.

Once again, Wat entered the clearing slowly, wary of startling the falcons if they should be here again. They were
nowhere to be seen, so he made his way over to his watching spot and stretched out along the forest floor, using a
root to keep his head out of the slightly damp earth. He
turned his gaze up to the blue sky and waited.

He had slept poorly last night, worried about curses and
bullies and the coming long winter. When he had finally
fallen asleep, he slept fitfully, dreaming of meat hooks and
a blacksmith who hammered meat pies until they disappeared.

He wiggled a bit, settling himself more comfortably into
the ground. A large white cloud floated overhead, and he
was struck by how closely it resembled Pig. As the cloud

moved on, a dark shape appeared, its graceful movements unmistakable. The falcon had returned. Just as Wat had hoped.

As it drew closer, Wat saw that it carried something in its talons. Letting out a high-pitched *kik, kik, kik,* the bird approached the clearing. An answering cry sounded high above Wat. He tilted his head back and saw that it came from the very tree he was leaning against. He held his breath, afraid of so much as twitching a muscle and disturbing the birds. He shifted his gaze up to the branches above him, where he could make out another falcon. This one was larger, probably a female, slate gray on top and striped underneath. A peregrine!

The falcon flew from the branch she'd been waiting on and went to join her mate in the air. As she approached him, she twisted around onto her back, stretching out her talons. The male bird flew straight toward her, coming so fast and true that Wat was afraid they would collide. At the last possible second, the male pulled back slightly and extended his talons. In a spectacular midair pass, the male handed off the prey it had been carrying and kept on flying. The female, the prey now in her talons, glided to a tree across the clearing and came to rest on a branch. She paused, casting her guarded gaze across the clearing. Finally satisfied that there was no immediate threat, she began to rip and tear the feathers from the dead bird. Now and again her alert eyes turned to search the horizon. When she had managed to pluck the carcass clean, she fluttered back to the oak tree with the prey dangling from her talons, then disappeared into a hollow Wat hadn't noticed before.

Wat closed his eyes, awed by the beauty and grace he had just witnessed. He tried to imagine himself, soaring high in the air, what it might feel like to have wind whooshing through a pair of wings. If he had the speed and strength of a falcon, he would—

Wat's thoughts were cut off by the sound of horses pawing the ground and jingling harnesses. Cheerful voices nearby erupted into laughter. Surprise and disappointment filled him. He had thought himself safe from prying Normans this deep into the forest. He scooted around to the back of the tree and rolled over onto his stomach so he could peer around the tree without being seen.

A group of maybe eight or nine mounted hunters stood in the clearing. Wat recognized Lord Sherborne and the shorter, bulky figure of Hugh, the master of the hunt. He shivered. Hugh was Sherborne's iron fist in the village; the one who saw to it that the new Norman laws were carried out, and administered the punishment when they weren't.

It was he and his men who patrolled the forests to keep poachers away.

It was he who set fire to the fields two years ago, burning the villagers' crops and turning houses into charred ash; who had flushed the refugees from the safety of the forest, straight into starvation and the arms of death.

It was he who had caught John Thatcher and brought him forth to be hanged.

Wat had hoped he'd used up all his bad luck yesterday morning, but it wasn't looking that way. Slowly, trying to keep from drawing any attention to his movements, he pulled back into his hiding place.

Lord Sherborne's slightly nasal voice broke through the quiet. "Where did you say you spotted them?"

"They flew in this way, my lord." Hugh dismounted and walked away from the group of men.

Wat watched through the tall grasses as Hugh studied the trees. He knew by the look of satisfaction that crossed the other man's face that he had spotted the small pigeon feathers littering the ground.

"Their nest must be nearby," he muttered. In a wide arc, he circled the clearing, examining the ground at the base of each tree, looking for more telltale droppings and feathers. He passed out of sight and Wat held his breath, hoping he wouldn't discover the bird's hollow.

"Aha!" he heard Hugh exclaim with a note of triumph in his voice.

Wat felt a rough hand on the back of his tunic as he was jerked to his feet.

"What are you doing here, boy?" Hugh asked, his rough voice demanding an answer.

"Nothing." Wat looked down at his dangling feet to keep from seeing the harsh accusations in the other man's eyes. "I've done nothing—sir. I was just resting beneath the tree. That's all."

Hugh studied Wat as if he were something disgusting he had managed to step in. "It wasn't you who ate them two plums whose pits we found a way back, was it?"

Wat looked up at Hugh in surprise.

The hunter tightened his grip, and Wat could feel his tunic bunched up around his neck as tight as a hangman's noose.

"Did you think I wouldn't see? It's what I live for. Tracking vermin like you." Hugh shook him for good measure. "That was fruit from his lordship's orchard, wasn't it? Do I need to remind you that's thieving, boy?"

Wat was saved from answering when Lord Sherborne called out, "What have you caught there, Hugh?"

"Nothing," Hugh called back over his shoulder. "Just a beggar brat that belongs to one of the kitchen maids."

He turned back to Wat. "Come with me and be still, or I'll make you sorry."

Wat had no doubt this was true. He had seen with his own eyes the cruelty and harshness these Normans were capable of. He limped along behind Hugh as they returned to the hunting party. Lord Sherborne ignored him completely, as if he didn't exist. Two of the knights acted as if they would catch Wat's deformities if he got too close, and made the sign of the cross as he passed them.

Placing Wat between himself and one of the other huntsmen, Hugh took up position in front of the horses. At his signal, one of the bowmen knelt and aimed his bow. Bitter disappointment seized Wat as he realized they had found the nest. The bowman loosed the arrow and it soared, straight and true, up into the oak tree.

The assault on the nest brought the female peregrine screeching from the hollow in attack. The moment she cleared the tree, Lord Sherborne released a huge gyrfalcon that had been sitting on his arm. The enormous bird of prey flapped its great wings and launched itself into the air.

The peregrine was one of the fastest of the falcons and soared high into the air, trying to dodge the larger hawk. When she was nothing but a tiny black dot in the blue sky, she turned, dropping like a stone back toward the earth at breathtaking speed. Looping and swerving, she tried to dodge the gyrfalcon. It was useless. No bird could escape the gyrfalcon's powerful wings. Faster than the eye could see, the larger falcon struck the peregrine from the air with a muffled *thud*. It circled quickly around and caught her in its talons before returning to Sherborne's arm.

"There's my beauty," Lord Sherborne murmured to the falcon as he accepted the dead bird with his left hand. "What a good job you've done." He tossed the lifeless peregrine toward the base of the oak.

Wat was stunned. These men would even snatch the birds from the sky so they could control them. He'd known they were cruel, but these were falcons! Even the Normans had enough sense to prize these birds for their skill and beauty. In fact, they'd passed laws declaring that only nobility was allowed to own them. Why then had they killed such a magnificent bird?

"That's one," Wat heard Hugh mutter under his breath.

Wat heard a distant screech and looked up to see the male

falcon come to his mate's defense. "No!" Wat yelled. The huntsmen grabbed him by the arm and boxed his ears.

The great gyrfalcon rose once again and went after the small peregrine male. Even with only one good eye, Wat could see he was not the least bit tired from his first kill.

· · ·

HUGH TOSSED THE SECOND DEAD BIRD AGAINST THE BASE of the oak tree.

He turned to Wat, who stood shocked and numb. Hugh reached out and snatched him by the shoulder and pulled him away from the other huntsmen. "You're small and light." He bent close to Wat and pointed up at the oak tree. "See that hollow up there in the oak? That'll be their nest. I want those nestlings." He shoved Wat toward the tree. "You can get to them easier than most. Or maybe we just care less if you fall." Hugh chuckled at his own cleverness.

Wat stumbled forward, pausing over the bodies of the two falcons. He could scarcely believe them dead, for even now they were proud, noble.

"Why'd you have to kill them?" he whispered, almost to himself.

He flinched as a huge hand came down on the back of his head with a crack. "Don't question your betters! Those birds were his lordship's to kill. By the grace of King William, Lord Sherborne owns everything—the birds in the sky, the berries in the brambles, every blade of grass you stand on, even the air you breathe. You live, like those falcons, because he suffers you to live. Although that could change at any time. Like it did with them." Hugh jerked his head toward the falcon bodies.

"Besides," he continued, "the chances of us taming them down were nigh impossible. They'd have attacked us when we went after their young, and those talons of theirs can do serious damage to a man. Now get up there and get me those nestlings."

Staring up at the tree's branches, Wat hesitated. Nothing was safe from these harsh new masters. Nothing could stop them. Certainly not someone as small and weak as himself. But he wanted no part of this. More than anything, he wanted to be strong enough to resist this foul man and refuse to help.

Almost as if sensing his thoughts, Hugh leaned over and put his face close. Wat could see the man's rotting teeth and smell his fetid breath. "If you don't do what I tell you, I'll do the same thing to you that we do to young falcons. You know what that is, don't you?"

Afraid to speak, Wat merely shook his head.

His voice soft and gentle, as if he were describing something wondrous to behold, he said, "We sew their eyes shut."

Wat tried to pull away from this horror, but Hugh held tight and kept talking in his soft gentle voice. "We've got to break their spirit, see? We have to teach them that they live by our grace. Just like we did with you villagers.

"So we sew their eyes shut. Blind them to the world around them. They're too young to fly, and without flight or sight, they're helpless. All ours for the taking. And the breaking." Hugh laughed at his own little rhyme.

Wat felt any fight he might have had in him flee at this hideous threat. He thought of the needle being put to his flesh, of the darkness that would follow as his eye was permanently sealed. He shuddered. Without sight in either eye . . . his mind skittered away from that thought. He would do anything to save himself from that fate. And Hugh knew it.

Wat grasped the coarse burlap bag that Hugh held out to him, then took a reluctant step toward the tree. Hugh gave Wat a rough boost up to the first branch and stepped back.

With his heart sitting like a stone in his chest, Wat began climbing upward, using his arms to pull himself from branch to branch. His mind spun in circles as he hoped that some answer or solution would come to him, but none did. In the end he had no choice but to fetch the nestlings.

When he drew even with the hollow, he jiggled the branch to test its sturdiness, then hoisted himself onto it. He risked a look down, then wished he hadn't. It was even farther than he had thought. He turned his attention back to the small hollow in the tree and peered in at the young peregrines.

They were two of the oddest-looking creatures he'd ever seen, especially when compared to their sleek parents. They were scrawny and awkward, like very bony, plucked chickens that had been re-covered in white fluff. They sat on some odd bits of straw and leaves, their dark, keen eyes watching his approach warily.

As he reached into the nest, the birds became a hissing, spitting mass of tiny sharp talons and vicious little beaks. Wat jerked his hand back in surprise. They were defending themselves! Against him!

"Don't stand there gawking! Bring 'em down," Hugh called out.

Trying to avoid the needle-sharp talons and beaks that were doing their best to rip his hands to shreds, Wat reached into the hollow. He grabbed the closest bird and popped it into the sack, trying to ignore the fierce pain that shot through him when its talons made contact with his hand. The second bird put up just as big a fight, and by the time he had them both in the sack, blood was oozing from the rips and tears in his hand.

He shifted his weight and began the climb down. The two small birds in the bag were surprisingly heavy, and Wat had to struggle to keep his footing while hanging on to the bag. He reached the lowest branch of the tree, and before he even stepped onto the ground, Hugh grabbed the bag from his hands. Wat dropped to the ground empty-handed, wincing slightly as his bad foot made contact.

"For your help today, I'll say nothing to the lord of your stealing his fruit. But I've got my eyes on you, boy. And you'd better not let me catch you in the forest again. You're up to no good here. I can smell it." He winked one of his small piggish eyes at Wat, then turned and headed back to the hunting party.

Wat stood, still as stone, his anger and frustration nearly choking him as he watched them ride out of the clearing. The one thing he didn't need was one more person trying to make his life unbearable. Ralph and the village bullies were already doing a fine job of it. The thought of Hugh watching him, tracking him, made Wat's stomach pitch and roll.

Trapped. He was as trapped as those nestlings. There was no place for him to go. The village wasn't safe, not with its taunting and bullies. Men who had no sense of what it offered had just taken the forest from him. Was his life to be spent in one long endless span of lurking in the shadows of the stable? Waiting for his mother to bring him scraps when she could? Raking out muck for all eternity?

He turned and looked at the motionless falcons, lying on the ground. Grief at the senseless loss of their life welled up inside him. He knelt down and pulled them into his lap. Stroking their soft slate gray feathers, he studied them, committing their form, their color, the very majesty of their being to his memory. It was the only thing he could think of to honor their passing.

When he could think of no more tributes or farewells to whisper, he gently laid the birds on the ground and turned toward the tree. Using his bare and bleeding hands, he dug deep into the dark, loamy earth, ignoring the new scrapes that appeared. Hot tears watered the ground where he worked, but he didn't stop until the grave was big enough and deep enough for the two birds to lie side by side, as they had died.

He carefully laid the two peregrines in the ground. He thought of their courage and strength, their fierce pride.

How they had died fighting, even against overwhelming odds. They had not hidden in the shadows; they had not run from their enemies. They had met their fate head-on. Wat hesitated for a moment, then plucked one flight feather from each bird.

As he held the feathers, his hands tingled and a sharp pain jolted through his head. The light around him suddenly grew brighter, clearer. He closed his eyes to let the pain pass, and when he opened them again, everything seemed normal once more. He shook it off. Hunger, fatigue, anger. All of these could make one's head swim. All of them together were sure to.

He looked back down at the birds in the grave he had prepared for them. He would learn from these birds. He would use these feathers to remind him of their strength, and he would try to be strong, like them. He tore a strip of cloth from his tunic, wrapped the feathers together, and then wove them into a side lock of his hair.

Reaching out for a handful of dirt, Wat sprinkled the earth over the falcons' bodies, repeating the process until they were completely buried. Standing, he tamped the ground hard with his foot, wanting to make sure they stayed covered. Staring at the small grave he had fashioned, he dropped to his knees and promised, "I will always remember."

His mind filled with the image of these proud birds in flight. The care the female had taken when feeding her young. The fearless way the male had rushed to his death, avenging his mate. Their young who had been taken captive and would now be dependent on man for all things.

Whose eyes would be sewn shut.

To tame them down.

To break their spirit.

Who would never be allowed to soar free, except at others' pleasure.

A hot fury burned inside him, leaving but one thought, like a glowing ember in his head. He slammed his fist into the ground.

"I will not let them do this!" He laid both his hands on the fresh grave and looked up to the sky.

"I swear it."

chapter
· 4 ·

Trying to take in great big gulps of air as quietly as possible, Wat approached the small building where the falcons and hawks were kept. He had run the entire way from the clearing, his fear for the nestlings giving speed to his tired legs.

He sidled up to the single window on the west side of the mews and strained to listen. His ears, sharper than most to compensate for his poor sight, could hear Hugh's voice murmuring instructions to the assistant falconer.

"They're young enough that they shouldn't give you too much trouble. Just tie on the jesses and leashes. When I get back from the hall, I'll show you how to sew their eyes shut. Then we'll walk them about."

As Hugh strode out of the building, Wat flattened himself against the wall, his throat nearly closing in panic at the thought of Hugh catching him here, now. To Wat's way of thinking, there was nothing on earth more evil than Hugh and the tasks he carried out for Lord Sherborne. Wat's fingers twitched as Hugh walked by his hiding place on his way to dine in the great hall, and Wat was surprised to find them make the sign to ward off evil. He'd never done that before.

Very quietly, as if he were nothing more than a light breeze, Wat moved from the wall to the doorway. When his eye adjusted to the semidarkness inside, he made out several perches of different heights occupied by birds of prey. He recognized the merlins, the kestrels, and a goshawk, but saw no sign of the gyrfalcon that had so ruthlessly killed the peregrines. Then he remembered the rumors he'd heard that it slept in Sherborne's private chambers in the manor house. Perhaps they were true.

A faint movement caught his eye as the keeper took one of the young peregrines out of the sack. Soothing its ruffled feathers, he placed the bird on a small table. The keeper crooned to the young bird as he tied a thin strip of leather to its foot, then tied the other end of the leash to a small perch. When he was certain the bird was well secured, he let go of it long enough to tie on two smaller strips of leather. These strips sported tiny bells that jingled, and the young falcon squawked as they were fastened to him.

"Yes, yes, I know. You'll get used to it, I'll wager."

The bird kept on squawking and nipped at the keeper's hand with its sharp little beak.

"Ah, hungry, are we? Well, you'll be hungry for a while, that you will." The small bird pecked at him one more time before he was placed on a perch. "Mind your manners," he teased the nestling. "We'll not feed you till you begin to learn some respect."

Wat clenched his fist, enraged that anyone would think these noble creatures could be reduced to such a state. He wished he were strong enough to march in there and tie that clodpoll of a keeper to one of those perches. Then he'd decorate him with tiny bells and leashes and see how he cared for it.

Impatiently, Wat watched the keeper repeat the process with the second bird, who was even less docile than the first and put up more of a fight. The man was in a fine lather by the time he'd finished with the second bird. He placed the agitated nestling on the perch next to its sibling and went to quiet the other birds, who had become unsettled by all the commotion.

Wat's leg ached from all his running, and the stitch in his side wouldn't go away. He shifted his weight to relieve the ache slightly, then froze at the crunching sound of the gravel under his feet. His heart thumped in his chest and he made ready to run. But the assistant keeper never paused in his duties and gave no sign that he had heard anything amiss.

Just as Wat despaired of him ever turning from the birds, the man wandered over to a small table and poured himself a tankard of ale. Drinking deeply, he eyed the birds. He put the tankard down and wiped his mouth with the back of his hand. "It'll be a long night with the likes of you," he muttered, examining his nipped finger. "You'll not tame as easy as they're hoping. Might as well grab some sleep while I can." He shook his head and went to lie down on the pallet.

Wat waited another eternity until he heard the heavy, deep breathing that told him the keeper was asleep. He shifted from his spot in the shadows and silently approached the young birds. He paused behind their blocks to give them time to adjust to his presence. Using small movements, he took an old, nicked hunting dagger from his belt and moved toward the jesses. Holding the bells quiet, he cut them from the birds and lay them on the floor next to the burlap sack the keeper had carelessly left there.

Wat's dagger hovered just above the leash. His own vow rang in his ears as he pictured the falcons' bright eyes being sewn shut. He steadied himself and reached out with his knife, slicing through the small leather straps. He moved so quietly, the nestlings didn't even realize they were free. "I'm sorry, little ones," he whispered, his voice no more than a lifting of the air around them. "It'll just be for a bit." With that apology, he reached for them. His breath caught at the downy softness of their feathers, the fragile feel of their bones. As carefully as he could, he laid them in the bottom of the burlap sack.

The other birds began to fuss, and Wat realized that speed would be more valuable than silence. He darted quickly for the door, startling the birds even more, so that the mews was a-squawk with the sound of unsettled falcons. Wat was out the door before the ruckus roused the sleeping man on the pallet. He awoke, springing to his feet in confusion, unsure of the cause of the commotion.

With any luck, it would take the keeper a while to figure out exactly what was missing. It would give Wat just enough time for the head start he would need. He knew he couldn't run faster than the others, but maybe, just maybe, if fortune's star would shine down on him just this once, he could stick to the shadows and they wouldn't be able to see his flight.

chapter

· 5 ·

HE RAN UNTIL HE COULD RUN NO MORE, THEN HE TROT-
ted. When his leg ached and throbbed so badly he thought
it would surely fall off, he slowed to a walk but still kept
moving deeper into the forest. His chest felt as if it were
weighted down with stones as he struggled for breath. Dusk
was all around him, and he knew night would arrive quick
and sudden, like a giant snuffing out a candle.

The cramped muscles in his arm burned and twitched.
Wat would never have guessed that two such weightless balls
of downy fluff could become such a burden. He switched
the bag to his other hand, worry settling over him as he realized how quiet and still they'd become. He needed to find
a safe place to stop for the night and check on them.

He had been careful to pick out a path leading south,
away from the clearing where Hugh had found him this
morning. It had been hours since he left the mews and not
once did he see any signs of pursuit. But deep down in his

heart he knew they would follow him. If not today, tomorrow. If not then, the following day.

The sky darkened from dusk to early nightfall, and Wat's progress slowed even more. Roots and stones rose up in his path, twisting around his feet or blocking his way. His only comfort was that the search parties would be hampered by nightfall even more than he. The forest had always been his place, his refuge from the ugliness of the manor and village life. But tonight it seemed different somehow. While he didn't quite fear it as the villagers did, he found himself with a new respect for the dangers that lurked in its darkened shadows. His one good eye peered through the gathering blackness, trying to locate a safe place to pass the night. Somewhere that offered a bit of protection from the wild boars, wolves, and bears that prowled among the trees at night. A cave, perhaps.

Food. They would also need food. Already it was too dark to search out anything to eat. And the young falcons would need meat. In his haste, he hadn't thought to bring anything to hunt with. No bow. No spear. Nothing but an old, nicked dagger that was practically useless for any type of hunting. And how often did the young birds need to eat? Did they need water? How much? How did he get it to them?

He should have taken the time to make some sort of plan.

Wat's foot caught on something once again, but this time he lost his balance and the ground came rushing up, knocking his breath clear out of him as he sprawled facedown on the forest floor. The bag holding the young falcons flew out of his hand, landing on the ground in front of him. He gasped and wheezed, his mouth working like a blacksmith's bellows as it tried to get air back into his burning lungs.

When at last he could breathe again, he sat up and felt along his arms and legs. While no bones were broken, his good ankle had been badly twisted during the fall. Testing it, he realized it wouldn't support his full weight. Now his good leg was as useless as his crippled one. Disgusted, he brushed the twigs from his tunic, plucked a bit of leaf out of his nose, and tried to take stock of his surroundings.

It was full dark now. Not wanting to put any weight on his twisted ankle, he crawled forward to where he thought the sack had landed, groping in the dark until his hand closed around the rough burlap. He pulled the sack close, then crawled over to the nearest tree and positioned himself in front of it. If he was stuck spending the night out in the open forest, he wanted something solid at his back.

He pulled the sack up close and peered in to check on the nestlings. They were silent and still, but two pairs of small, bright eyes looked back at him. With one finger, he reached out to pet their fluffy down. It was so soft, he could scarcely be sure he was touching it.

"I'm sorry," he murmured to the birds. "I didn't plan well—'tis a fault of mine, this not planning," he confessed. "I don't have any meat for you, but I will tomorrow, I promise. As soon as it is light enough, I will find something to—oh! I forgot." He reached his hand down to his pocket, pleased to discover the lump of meat pie still sitting there from yesterday. "Here's something you'll like," he told the birds. "The best meat pasties, straight from his lordship's table."

He held the birds in place with one hand while he dug around in his pocket with the other. Two pairs of bright eyes watched him closely.

The pie was squashed, with meat filling oozing out the sides in places. Wat pinched a bit of the filling and held it out in front of the nestlings.

Uncertain, the larger one cocked her head and studied the glob of meat. The smaller one, the male, had no such caution and lunged forward and nipped the meat off Wat's finger.

"Ow!" Wat yelped, then hastened to get another bite ready as the young nestling prepared to stab again. After a few more assaults on his fingers, Wat decided to rip the pie open and expose the filling for them to peck directly off the crust. The nestlings seemed unsure what to do, until Wat held the pie out and slightly above him at about the same angle he reckoned a mother bird would have.

After watching the other bird for a bit, the larger nestling finally decided to risk it and made a stab for the filling clinging to the pie shell.

Wat watched in satisfaction as these two wild creatures ate from his hand. He would never have imagined such a thrill. For the first time in his life, something needed him. He could provide for them, keep them safe. And not because he wanted to own them or control them, but because he wanted to give them a chance to be free.

In surprisingly little time the meat pie was plucked clean, leaving nothing but an empty shell of pastry crust that the birds refused to eat. Wat pulled off a piece of the crust and stuffed it in his mouth. The birds watched, curious. Once they realized there were no more meat bits, they began running their beaks through their feathers, as if combing them. They sat together in a companionable silence, Wat eating bits of day-old pastry for his dinner and enjoying the sensation of two wild things settling in his lap.

When every last crumb of the pie was gone, Wat gave a deep sigh as a sense of peacefulness settled over him.

"Good night," he whispered to the nestlings, then gently placed them back in their sack. "I will watch over you. I promise." Wat finished reassuring the birds, pulled the sack back over their heads, then brought it up snug against his body to keep them as warm as possible throughout the long night.

The night was so dark now that Wat could barely make out the shape of the nearest trees. The earthy green smell of the forest floor rose up, familiar and reassuring. As his tense muscles began to unwind, he found he was quite comfortable. His hair lifted as the cool night air brushed past his cheek. He yawned, then shook himself. He would keep watch over the young falcons as they slept.

He heard a small rustle in the undergrowth, but pushed aside his worry. Such a small noise was nothing to be afraid of. An owl hooted nearby, and was answered by a second owl, farther off.

Wat's thoughts went to the corner of the stable where he usually slept, burrowed in the old straw. He realized he was just as comfortable here, propped up against the tree. At least here he was sheltered from prying eyes and thick-skulled spit-turners with foul tempers.

When he was very young, he had slept with his mother and the other maidservants in the women's quarters. He remembered how safe he had felt in her embrace, her body warm as she cuddled against him on cold nights, her comforting whispers heard only by him. She had created a special world for him in her arms, one that pain and shame had no part in. In his eighth year, the other serving women had complained that he was too old to stay in their quarters any longer. The pain of that day still cut like a knife; the anguish of being cast out, away from his mother's side. He knew she argued against it. He'd heard her himself as he hid in the shadows behind closed doors. But her arguments had fallen on deaf ears.

His mother had helped him find a small corner in the stable, one that no one would object to. That had been his home ever since, the gentle snorting and blowing of Pillock and the donkeys replacing his mother's lullabies. But he savored the memory, and on nights like this, when he was cold and alone, he took it out and wrapped it around himself like a warm blanket.

. . .

WAT WAS RUNNING. HIS TWISTED FOOT DRAGGED USELESS behind him. Sweat dripped into his one good eye, blurring his vision. They were getting closer. So close. The ground shook with the force of their running. He heard their heavy breathing drawing closer, almost in his ear. Or was it his own ragged breath as he struggled for air? His side ached so much, he feared it was splitting. His bad foot was so heavy, he feared he couldn't lift it again to go another step. But he must. Or they would catch him.

His whole body shuddered as he felt a hand on his shoulder.

He jerked awake and blinked a couple of times. The sky was dark still, the moon not yet risen. Only a few stars shone in the sky, casting everything around him into shades of dark gray and black. Where was he? The forest! He stiffened as he remembered. He had dreamed that someone touched his shoulder. Straining his ears, he listened, yet heard nothing. He turned his head and peered into the darkness, past the dark silhouette of a slender tree stump with a branch reaching out in his direction. Maybe that was it. Maybe he had merely bumped against the branch in his sleep.

As the dream finally cleared from his vision, he saw a soft flickering of red light. He sat up, instantly alert. A small fire had been lit nearby, the embers glowing. He froze. A fire could mean only one thing.

His heart leaped to his throat when a dry, whispering voice came floating out of the trees.

"Don't you know the dangers of sleeping in the open forest at night?"

SLOWLY, STIFFLY, THE STUMP BEGAN TO UNFOLD ITSELF. Other branches began to move and flap around, and Wat realized they were two arms and two legs covered in a rough, brownish-gray cloak. The top portion of the stump turned. With shock, Wat found himself staring into a pair of deep gray eyes that sat in a heavily lined face, the lower half of which was covered by a long, gray beard.

This, Wat thought, this was what came of sleeping out in the open forest unguarded. He eyed the stranger warily.

The old man turned back to the fire and poked at the flames with a stick. "Well, don't you understand the dangers, young fool?"

Wat finally found his tongue. "I'm not afraid of anything here in the forest."

The old man snorted. "We all have something to fear." He threw Wat a sly look. "Some more than others."

Wat tried to study the old man in the faint light. He'd never seen him before, not in the village, nor on any of his trips into the forest. He was certain he'd remember if he'd seen that face before. And he'd never heard any tales of an old hermit who lived in these woods. "Who are you?" he blurted out.

"Who am I? Who am I? he asks." The old man cocked his head at Wat. "Well, who are *you?*"

Wat opened his mouth to answer, then thought better of it. It wasn't just himself anymore. He had two others who were counting on him. He pulled the sack closer to his body.

"See," the old man cackled. "It's not so easy a question to answer now, is it?"

Stung to words, Wat said, "I'm just a lad."

"From the village?"

Wat thought about how to answer that. Would it give away too much if the man knew where he had come from?

The old man barked out a laugh. "Of course you came from the village! If you were from the forest, I'd have known about you before now. Why would you not want me to know that?" A look crossed the old man's face, and his whole body changed, growing larger, more threatening. His eyes bored into Wat. "You weren't responsible for those two deaths earlier today, were you? Over in the oak grove?"

How did he know? Wat wondered. Had he been

watching from the trees? "No!" Wat said. "I'm trying to make up for those deaths."

"How can anyone make up for such brutality?" the man asked.

Wat stuck his chin out stubbornly. "I can try."

The old man cocked his head, as if Wat had finally said something truly interesting. "That you can. So, who *are* you, then, lad?"

"Just a lad from the village, like you said."

The old man took the stick he'd been poking at the fire and pulled it out of the flames. He held the burning tip closer to Wat and looked him up and down, seemingly through to his very soul.

Wat endured his scrutiny in silence, not wanting to give the man cause to think he was guilty of any wrongdoing. The man's outrage over the falcons' death gave Wat hope that he wouldn't be handing him over to Lord Sherborne or Hugh come morning.

After looking long and hard at Wat's face and his misshapen eye, the man finally spoke. "Did they tell you your father was the devil?"

Wat looked up in shock. "Aye. They did. But how did you know?"

Slowly the old man shook his head. "They used to tell

me the same thing. I'll wager it is no truer for you than it was for me." Slowly, he pulled his cloak back from his head, just far enough to expose his left ear, which was shrunken and misshapen like a dried mushroom.

"Oh," was all Wat could think of to say. It was the first time he'd ever met anyone who had a deformity such as his. Who had most likely lived through the same types of torment as he had. "Does it hamper your hearing?" he finally asked.

"Eh?"

Wat leaned forward and spoke louder. "I said, does it hamper your—"

"No, no," the old man said, waving his hand and chuckling. "'Twas a joke." The old man motioned with his hand for Wat to lean closer. "Now here's a secret I'll share with you." He pointed a finger at Wat's eye, then his own ear. "These aren't signs of the devil." He leaned closer and whispered, "They're signs we were born under fortune's star."

Wat stiffened, studying the man more carefully. "That's what my mother always told me." Surprise caused him to say the words out loud, even though he had told himself to keep silent so that the stranger would be on his way as quickly as possible. Who was this man that used the same words that his mother did?

"Did she?" The old man paused and turned his gaze back to Wat. He leaned forward and took Wat's chin between his thumb and finger, turning his face this way and that.

"Your mother used to say? Is she dead, then?" he asked. Something deep within the old man grew still as he waited for the answer.

"No. She's alive."

The old man held even more still. "And tell me, boy, what is your mother's name?"

Again, Wat paused to think if this could make more trouble for him, but the look on the old man's face was burning in its intensity.

"Brenna. Brenna is my mother's name," he answered, almost against his will, as if the words had somehow been called from him.

The stick he'd been poking at the flames with fell out of the old man's hand, and he closed his eyes, as if he'd just experienced some great pain he could hardly bear.

Wat watched, concerned. What was wrong with him? Was he having a seizure of some sort? And what should Wat do about it if he was?

The old man finally opened his eyes and cleared his throat. "Brenna, you say?"

Wat nodded. "Do you know her?"

"Describe her to me."

Wat wanted to argue, but there was a desperation in the man's voice, a sense of need so strong that it pulled Wat along with it. "She is slight of build, not much taller than me. Her hair is red, her skin pale, and her eyes are moss green."

As Wat spoke, the man brought his hand up to his chest and began rubbing it over his heart, as if something inside of him ached. "By the gods," he finally whispered, his voice faint.

Wat could stand it no longer. "Are you ill? Can I get you something?"

The man held up his hand and shook his head. "No, I'll be fine in a minute. Tell me more of your mother."

Torn between his desire to keep silent and his fear for the old man, Wat found himself saying, "She works in the manor kitchens, for Lord Sherborne."

"She is well and happy?"

Wat had never considered this before. He knew she was well enough, but happy? And what business was it of this nosy old man's? "Why do you want to know so much about my mother?" he finally asked. "What business is it of yours?"

The old man gave Wat a long, studied look, opened his

mouth to answer, then changed his mind. "Never mind. So tell me, what have you got in the sack there? Food, perhaps? Ale?"

Wat looked down at the sack in his lap. What would this man do if he knew of the young birds? He'd been furious at what was done to the falcons earlier. Did that mean Wat's secret would be safe with him? Would he be able to help somehow? "No," Wat answered slowly. "No food."

The old man raised one of his bushy eyebrows. "Well, what is it, then?"

Once again, Wat hesitated. He was eager to turn the talk from his mother, but could he trust this man? Something deep inside him said yes. Wat had never seen him in the village, so it was unlikely he would go there now, just to turn Wat in. And once he realized that Wat had rescued the nestlings from the very men who had killed the other falcons, surely he would understand. "Well, remember how I told you earlier I was trying to amend those deaths you spoke of?"

The man nodded his head.

"These are their young. The nestlings. Lord Sherborne and his men killed the parents so they could get to the nestlings."

"And how do you come to have them?" The old man eyes narrowed with suspicion.

"I snuck into the mews and . . . and took them," Wat explained.

Wat had his full attention now. "You went into their midst and snatched them from under their nose?"

Wat squirmed nervously on the hard ground. "Aye."

The old man threw back his head and laughed with glee. "Oh, well done, lad. Well done."

A pleasant warmth blossomed through Wat at these words of praise, and he found himself glad he'd decided to trust the stranger.

"However," the old man said as he stopped laughing, "you've also landed yourself in the middle of a fine mess."

"I had to save them. I couldn't leave them to that hunting party. Do you know what they do to young falcons back there?"

"Oh, yes. I do. I know exactly how they treat wild things up at the manor."

"Besides," Wat continued, more calmly now, "their parents died trying to protect them. I couldn't let their deaths be for nothing." For some reason, it seemed vitally important to him that the old man understand.

"Now there's a question for you. Can a death mean nothing? I think not, boy."

Wat sighed in frustration. "I shouldn't have hoped you'd understand."

"Oh, I understand all right. Probably more than you. I understand that it is parents' nature to protect their offspring, no matter what the cost to themselves. If the old must die so the young must live, so be it. It is the way of things." The old man leaned even closer to Wat. "But the reason I don't despair as you do is because I understand that the essence of those falcons will not fade."

"What do you mean, 'essence'?" Wat asked.

The old man reached through his beard and scratched his chin. "Think of it this way. In early winter, when the pond first ices over, is it any less water than before?"

Wat shook his head.

"No, of course not. It's still water, but frozen water. Then, if you take a piece of that ice and boil it in a pot, it becomes water again and then something else, right, boy?"

Wat cocked his head and waited for the answer, curious in spite of himself.

"And do you know what it becomes?" the old man asked him.

Wat shook his head.

"Vapor! Water vapor, to be precise. One essence, three forms. For you see, even though the form changes, the essence remains the same. Do you understand, boy?"

"I think so," Wat replied cautiously. "So, what is the new form the peregrines have taken?"

The old man smiled at Wat. "That is a question I cannot answer." The old man sighed. "Have you given any thought to your mother? What she might be suffering on account of your actions?"

Wat felt a small shiver across his neck. "But why would she be suffering?" he asked.

"Use that thick head of yours, boy. She'd be worried about you, for one. And Sherborne might punish her for your thievery."

Wat's mouth dropped open. "I never even thought of that."

"No. Of course you didn't."

Wat would have liked to argue the point, but felt the ring of truth in the stranger's words. The small fire was cold now, and the old man lapsed into silence, twirling the end of his beard with his finger. He looked up as dawn was just beginning to lighten the sky. "'Tis a good omen, to begin a journey in the between times, when it is neither light nor dark, day or night," he muttered to himself, then creaked to a standing position.

Wat opened his mouth to speak.

"Never mind." He dismissed Wat's unspoken question with a wave of his hand. "What's done is done. You'd best stay with me till it's all forgotten." He turned on his heel and began walking out of the clearing.

Wat stood up, carefully cradling the nestlings in the bag. Something deep inside him had decided to trust this man. His outrage on behalf of the birds was equal to Wat's own, and his dislike for the people of the village seemed almost as strong. Maybe Wat could find shelter with him. The birds needed to be somewhere safe. Perhaps this musty old hermit had a cave somewhere, one he'd be willing to share with Wat and the birds. Reminding himself that it wasn't only himself any longer, Wat made his decision and shouldered the bag. As he fell into step behind the stranger, he asked, "How long do you think it will be till the whole thing is forgotten?"

"Years, boy, years," the old man replied. "You're not easily forgotten once you've been seen."

chapter

· 7 ·

THEY WALKED ON, THE OLD MAN SAYING NOTHING AND staying just far enough ahead of Wat to make conversation impossible. They went deeper into the forest, picking out a path where there was none and venturing farther than Wat had ever dared on his own. The trees, taller, thicker, more gnarled, seemed like ancient sentinels standing guard over the secrets of the woods.

As the sun burned off the morning mists that swirled about their feet, Wat's thoughts turned to the young birds who lay so quiet in the sack. They needed food and water. Wat needed to go hunting for them, somehow.

Near midmorning they came to a cottage that was so old and broken-down it looked as if the forest had begun to reclaim it. Vines crawled over the chimney and covered the thatched roof while ivy grew unchecked up its walls.

"Do you live here?" asked Wat when he caught up to the old man at last.

"When it suits me," was his reply. He pushed open the

door of the cottage, which immediately collapsed to the floor, stirring up a storm of dust and cobwebs.

Wat sneezed and waved his hand in front of his face, trying to chase away the worst of the dust. "And when was the last time it suited you?" he asked dryly.

"Not for a while," the old man admitted. He walked over to peer up the chimney. "We'd better check for nests before we light the fire," he commented.

Once the dust had settled, Wat looked about the room. In one corner there was a small bed with a sagging straw mattress. A large, rough table that looked as if it had been fashioned from a fallen tree stood in the center of the room. Beside the table were two equally rough benches.

Against the wall, wobbly-looking shelves held chipped pieces of crockery and earthenware jars. Wat thought if he shouted, or perhaps even sneezed again, the whole thing would tumble to the floor. A fine dusting of cobwebs covered all.

"Don't just stand there gawking," the old man called out to Wat. "Come see what fate has delivered into our hands."

Wat moved over to where the old man stood. He stared down at the fallen door, which had landed on a rather large mouse.

"Dinner," said the old man.

Wat looked up at him, horrified.

"Not ours, you young fool! For your falcons. If they've not eaten in a while, they will greatly appreciate this tender morsel. Find them a makeshift nest for now, then go fix them their meal."

Wat looked around the room. There was an old wooden bucket with a plank missing. No good for carrying water, but it would make a fine tree hollow. He picked it up and held it out for the old man's inspection. "Can I use this?"

"Certainly, certainly. I don't care what you use," the old man said absently, his attention still on the bed he was examining. "It's been a long time since these old limbs have slept in a bed," he mumbled. He reached down and tested the mattress. "Needs new stuffing." He turned back to Wat. "Go tend to your birds!"

The old man turned his back on Wat and began examining his pots and jars. "Valerian, skullcap, wormwood, yarrow," he muttered to himself. "Yes, yes. All here as they should be." Without turning around, he called to Wat, "Do I have to light a fire under you?"

Wat stopped gawking at his surroundings. He carried the sack over to the bucket and reached for the young birds. Even when his hand reached into the sack, they made no noise or movement, and he feared the worst. When his fingers touched them, however, they stirred and made a feeble attempt to fend him off with their talons. One at a time he pulled them out of the bag, noticing their rumpled feathers. They certainly looked worse for wear. He laid the sack in the bucket for padding and placed the birds on top of it. "I'll hurry with your dinner, I promise," he whispered.

Wat gingerly picked up the mouse by its long tail and carried it outside. He'd never skinned an animal before. When hunting had still been permitted, he'd been too young, and now that he was old enough, hunting was forbidden. He sat down outside the cottage door, trying to figure out the best way to go about the task. He pulled out his knife and decided to cut the skin from the neck and scrape it off.

As his knife worked on the mouse, he mulled over the last few hours. Even though he hadn't started out with a plan, he needed to form one now. He needed to pay attention and not risk the young birds further. The shock at finding this odd man in the forest had left him confused and distracted. He'd expected to find himself alone, just him and the birds together, making do with what the forest provided, living on their own. But now there was another person to be dealt with. Someone who could offer them shelter and perhaps some protection, which he liked. Someone to tell him what to do and when, which he didn't care for a bit.

Once the mouse was skinned, he had to decide the best way to feed it to the nestlings. He closed his eyes and tried to imagine how the mother falcon would have done this. His mind filled with the image of her, back from the kill. She had held the prey still in her talons and ripped the feathers away with her sharp beak. She would most likely have done the same in order to tear the meat from the carcass.

Opening his eyes, he used the tip of his knife to pull small gobbets of meat from the mouse carcass. It was surprising how little meat there actually was on a plump mouse. He hoped it would be enough. It would certainly be better than nothing.

Back inside the cottage, the old man was nowhere to be seen. Relieved, Wat went over to the little falcons in the bucket. Seeing his approach, they lifted their talons in his direction. Wat smiled wryly at their efforts to defend their bucket against a one-eyed, cripple-footed boy. He hoped it was a sign their spirits hadn't been damaged by their adventures.

Wat sat down on the floor in front of the bucket. "Hush now. I'm just going to feed you, that's all." He held out a tiny strip of meat to the smaller one, who was hissing louder. The bird couldn't resist the morsel. He reached out with his razor-sharp little beak and grabbed for the meat. Wat could see the lump sliding down his throat as the bird swallowed. The falcon squawked for more before Wat had even given the second bird a piece.

"Not so interested in defending your territory now that I have food, are you, greedy one? Now wait your turn." He fed a strip to the second bird, who gobbled it down in the same way as the first and was immediately ready for another piece.

The mouse meat disappeared with surprising speed. "That's it, that's all there is," Wat told the birds. Wanting to make sure they understood, he held out his empty hands to show them. Apparently disbelieving, the smaller one pecked at Wat's finger.

"Ouch!" Wat snatched his hand back. "That's not meat! That's my thumb."

"Thumb. Meat. It's all the same to them," said the old man from the doorway. "Besides, I can see from here that their crops are full. They've had enough for now."

Wat leaned forward and noticed two small, pinkish pouches bulging out of the birds' throats that hadn't been there before.

"Leave the birds and come with me. We have much to do to make this cottage ready for nightfall."

Once again, Wat had to quicken his pace to keep up with the old man. His twisted foot ached from the distance they had already walked, but he forced himself to put the pain out of his mind.

"Where are we going?" he asked, trying to distract himself.

"To collect new mattress stuffing, for one. To see what we can find to eat, for another."

They walked until they came to a place where the forest floor was covered with leaves. The old man handed Wat an empty sack. "Your back is younger than mine. Pick up these leaves we'll need to stuff the mattress."

Wat reached up to a nearby tree. "Wouldn't these leaves be softer?"

Long, bony fingers clamped around Wat's wrist. "No." The old man's face was suddenly inches from his, frightening in its intensity. "You must never take leaves or branches from a tree without its permission."

"W-why?"

"Because a tree is a sacred thing. Besides," he said, motioning with his other hand, "there is plenty here on the ground, and that is good enough for me." He let go of Wat and moved away.

Wat stared at his wrist. The old man's touch had been dry

and rough . . . and something else. Something he couldn't name. Wat's skin felt as if it were humming where the old man had touched it.

Wat shook his head and began stuffing the leaves into the sack, keeping his eye on the old man as he did so.

The old man searched about on the ground, poking the soft earth with his walking stick. Not finding what he was looking for, he moved on to try again. "Aha!" he said at last. He bent over to pick something up. To Wat, it looked remarkably like an old pig snout. "Dinner!" the old man proclaimed.

Wat wasn't worried. "For the falcons."

"No! Of course not. Ours. They wouldn't eat it anyway."

Wat wasn't sure he would either. The old man looked up and saw Wat watching him. "A parsley root. It will be good boiled and mashed," he explained. He turned his attention back to the root, inspecting it closely, and asked, "Do you have any other family? A brother perhaps? Or a father?"

Wat shook his head. "My mother never spoke of my father. Whenever I asked she grew so saddened and upset that I stopped asking. The only thing I know is that he played her false." A flutter of shame and loss quivered in his chest. His mind scuttled away from the familiar pain of that subject, looking for something else to latch onto. He stopped gathering leaves as a thought occurred to him. "She did say I had a grandfather."

"Did she, now?" The old man dropped the root into his pocket. He folded both of his hands on the top of his staff and studied Wat. "And, what of him?"

Wat shrugged. "I don't know. He lived far away, where she said we couldn't go, so I've never met him." Wat smiled. "But my mother had stories she used to tell."

"And what did your mother tell you of him?"

"Well . . ." Wat thought a moment. "Mostly that he was very old and a little mad."

Wat glanced up at the old man. His great, thick eyebrows were drawn together in a frown. He looked both amused and annoyed. "Come," he said to Wat abruptly. "That should be enough mattress stuffing. We need to go tickle some trout. One parsley root won't fill our bellies worth spit." He turned and headed to where the shadows lengthened between the trees.

Wat fastened his bag and threw it over his shoulder, then followed. The thicker trees blocked the sun's rays, and gooseflesh popped up along his arms. He forced himself not to shiver.

"Do you smell it?" the old man whispered. He stopped walking and Wat nearly bumped into him.

"Smell what?" Wat sniffed. Something was different. He sniffed again. It smelled richer, cooler, damper. "Water?" he asked.

"Ha! Excellent!" The old man reached out and gave Wat a thump on the back. "Splendid, splendid!" He turned and continued on his way down the path. Wat followed, feeling somewhat like he had just passed a very important test. Of what, he wasn't certain, but he didn't mind. It was a pleasant feeling.

Before long the cheerful gurgling of a stream reached Wat's ears. "I can hear it," he ventured, hoping for more approval.

"Well, of course you can," answered the old man, not at all impressed. "You're half blind, not half deaf!"

Not quite knowing what to say, Wat kept silent.

Before long, the stream came into sight. The old man held his finger in front of his lips and motioned for Wat to sit on a nearby rock. He watched as the old man rolled up his sleeves and pulled the hem of his robe up through his legs and tucked it into his belt. Wat marveled at the spindly, white legs, wondering how the old man managed to get around on them. They reminded him of old knotted alder branches.

The old man walked down to the water's edge and

entered the stream without causing a single ripple. He took up a position in front of a large rock that cast a shadow over the water. He tossed his beard over his shoulder and then bent over, hands poised.

The old man held so still it was as if he had frozen. The shadowed grays of his hair and cloak blended in with the shadows cast by the trees and the silver water as it rushed over the rocks. He was difficult to see, and Wat had to blink to make sure he was still there. After watching for a while, Wat grew bored and stretched out on the rock, flexing his aching foot. He closed his eyes and listened to the sounds of the forest, trying to identify them all. It was a game he played often, a way to keep his hearing sharp. He heard the rustling of the leaves, grass being buffeted by the wind, the gurgling of the stream, the hum of an insect, and a loud *whoop!* Then a large splash. He jerked to a sitting position.

The old man sat waist-deep in the stream holding a giant trout in his hands. "Don't just sit there gawking! Come grab this cursed fish so I can get up!" Wat hurried over and took the slippery, wiggling fish from the gnarled hands. The old man pushed himself to his feet and stared down at his dripping robe in disgust. "Must've lost my balance," he muttered. "Too old for this sort of thing, really." He squelched his way to the stream bank and snatched the trout from

Wat's hands. "That's my dinner, boy. Now I'll sit in the sun while you go catch your own."

"Aren't you afraid of taking his lordship's fish?" Wat asked, more than a little nervous about doing just that.

His question was met with a snort of disgust. "Norman lords! Those brutes don't own that which lives here. These creatures belong to the earth, as they have for hundreds of years before these Normans came. Saying otherwise doesn't make it so."

Wat thought the Thatcher family might be tempted to disagree, but he was emboldened by the old man's words, so he rolled up his sleeves and got to work.

It took far longer for Wat to catch his trout. He tried to copy what he had seen the old man do, but there must have been some other secret to it. His sharper hearing was no help at all with the loud bubbling of the brook, and time and again his hands came up empty. When he was done, he was even wetter and grumpier than the old man had been, but at least he had his fish, even if it was small and probably the slowest fish in all of Britain.

The old man watched Wat emerge from the stream with a spark of approval in his eye. "You don't complain much, do you, boy?" he said at last.

Wat paused for a minute, aware of the icy water trickling

down his back and puddling between his toes. "I've never found it to do much good, is all."

The old man nodded. "True enough. Come, we've still much work to do before nightfall." He turned and headed back to the cottage.

As they reentered the shadow of the trees, Wat's damp flesh chilled instantly, and this time he couldn't help but shiver.

A thought occurred to him. "Do you have a name, or something, I could call you . . . ?" His words stumbled to a halt as the old man turned and fixed him with an unfathomable gaze. Wat saw all sorts of things he couldn't recognize flicker in the depths of the man's eyes. The old man regarded him for a full minute before he turned and continued walking.

"Well, now that you ask," he said over his shoulder, "Grandfather would do nicely, I think."

Wat's mouth dropped open in astonishment.

"But if you choke overmuch on that," the old man continued, walking on, "you can call me Griswold. And you'd best close your mouth before I mistake you for the trout you just caught and fix you for my supper."

chapter

· 8 ·

WAT COULDN'T FIND HIS TONGUE. "M-MY GRANDFATHER?"

"Yes, your mother's father, to be exact."

"But . . . she never talked about you."

The old man stopped again and turned around. "She didn't?"

"Well, only once or twice. And it was as if you were part of a story that had happened long ago."

Griswold turned and resumed walking. "And so it was."

Wat could scarcely believe his ears. All these years of being alone, of struggling to get by, just him and his mother, and there'd been someone else all along. Barely a stone's throw away. And amid all their suffering, his mother had rarely talked about him. Did she know that he still lived here—so deep and alone in the forest? Why didn't he ever come to the village? Wat had assumed the man was dead.

Wat quickened his pace to catch up to his grandfather. "How come I've never seen you before?"

"You've never come this far into the forest before," was the reply.

"But you could have come to the village to visit us," Wat persisted.

"I never knew you existed until a few hours ago."

"You didn't?" That felt better somehow. As if, maybe, he would have visited Wat if he'd only known. But how could he not know?

"I knew your mother was living in the village," Griswold continued. "Where else would she have gone? But she walked out on me, on our life. It was clear she wanted nothing more to do with me or our forest home, so I let it be. The time comes for the young to leave the nest. It was her time and I would not hold her back. Now," Griswold said, looking up at the horizon. "We must hurry so we can make ready for nightfall." He began walking faster.

Wat's mother had just walked out, with no explanation? Had she come to hate the forest, then? Now that Wat thought upon it, she had never ventured out into it with him, almost as if she had avoided it. But why?

Wat's questions followed him all the way back to the cottage. And while he knew they would not leave him, he tried to put them aside for the rest of the afternoon as he and

Griswold did what they could to make the cottage ready for the night. Besides, Wat was reluctant to do much thinking in Griswold's presence. The old man had an uncanny ability to sense his thoughts. It was probably safest to do his thinking in private.

His first chore was to empty the old stuffing out of the mattress and fill it with the new leaves while his grandfather, or Griswold, as Wat had decided to call him, retied the ropes on the bed. When Wat brought the freshly stuffed mattress back inside, he found the old man still struggling, his gnarled fingers fumbling helplessly with the stiff, coarse rope.

"Here, I'll do that if you like," Wat offered.

"Eh?" Griswold looked up in some confusion. "Aye. That would be good." He stared at his hands ruefully. "These don't seem to work as well as they once did." Wat knelt beside the bed frame and grabbed the end of a piece of rope while his grandfather went to study the door to see what it would take to get it back on its hinges.

Just as Wat got the last of the ropes retied, he looked up to find the old man struggling to wrestle the heavy door up off the floor. Wat hurried over and grabbed one end, and together they were able to hoist it to an upright position.

Griswold peered at him from around the side of the door. "You're a handy bit to have around, aren't you?"

Wat shrugged, but felt a warm glow of pleasure spread through him at being found helpful. All his life he'd been shooed away, dismissed as useless. He'd always known he could be helpful, if only someone would give him the chance. But no one ever had. Until now.

He stepped forward and used his back to hold the heavy door in place while Griswold tried to fix the decayed hinge. "There!" Griswold said at last, and stepped back to survey his handiwork. Wat stepped away from the door and turned to look. It hung crookedly and daylight showed all around.

Griswold snorted in disgust. "I'm no carpenter. But the nights are warm now. It's going to have to do."

Next, Griswold handed Wat a long branch, jagged and scarred on one end, with dried leaves still clinging to the other. "Birch," the old man explained, "knocked down by a storm some time ago, in case you're wondering. Use it for the cobwebs on the ceiling and shelves, as well as any other harmful things that lurk among the dust."

Wat hoped he meant spiders, but couldn't help feeling that he meant something else entirely, then decided he didn't want to know more. When he was finished, Griswold instructed him to use the branch to sweep the biggest bits of debris off the cottage floor.

Just when Wat was sure he was done, Griswold turned to him one more time. "Get those two buckets and take them back to the stream for filling. Your nose will lead you right to it."

Grateful for the chance to be alone, Wat picked his way through the trees, letting his thoughts wander as they would. He had a grandfather. To have a grandfather in his life was something he'd never imagined. His family consisted solely of himself and his mother. That was all there had ever been. He wasn't sure he needed more. And why had his mother told him that his grandfather lived too far away? Why did his mother never visit her father? Why had she run away? No matter how many times he asked the questions, he could find no answers.

When the stream came into view, he gladly put aside his thoughts and filled the buckets with the cool, clear water. When they were full, he set them down, knelt near the edge of the stream, and dipped his hands into the water to wash his face.

A fluttering motion caught his eye and he noticed the feather in his hair, reflected back by the water. Quickly, he averted his gaze, as he always did when confronted with his own reflection. But the stream called to him just as surely as if it whispered his name. There was no one to observe him looking at himself, no one to call out jests and crude remarks. For some reason, his reflection beckoned. Perhaps it was to see if he had changed somehow. If all that he had been through in the last day had changed him as much on the outside as he felt changed on the inside. Pulled by some force he could not name, Wat leaned over the water and looked.

There he was, reflected in the water. Slowly, his hand reached up to his face and his fingers traced the scarred, bruised flesh around his eye, the dark red skin that surrounded his pale, unseeing eye and caused people to cross themselves whenever he was near. He had been born this way, and no one knew why. That's why they blamed it on the work of the devil. His mother had told him that his birth had been long and difficult. Perhaps that is what had caused the deformity. He would never know. All he knew was that it had shaped his life since the day he was born, and no one had been able to see past it, except his mother, and now Griswold. They seemed to see it as a mark of favor.

He sighed and pushed himself to his feet. Maybe living in the forest, away from the townspeople, would be for the better. He wouldn't miss the pain of their cruel taunts and jeers. He had often longed to be free of their harsh judgments, their suspicions, and had looked forward to not having to wonder when the next boot heel or clenched fist would come his way. No, the only thing he would miss from the village was his mother, but between her duties in the kitchens and his home in the stable, their paths rarely crossed much, and when they did, it was always at great risk to her. He turned and headed back to the cottage.

"Ah! There you are," Griswold called out as Wat approached. "Here, I'll take those. Bring in the kindling, and while I start the fire, you can clean and gut our fish."

Wat handed Griswold the buckets and headed back outside. Cold, hungry, and fatigued, he found he was tired of being ordered around like a scullery maid. It was bad enough in the village, where anyone above him in station—everyone in the village—had the right. Here in the forest, where he'd imagined he'd be free, it bothered him more. He thought briefly of telling this to the old man, but a lifetime of training held him back. Instead, he set about his task. When his arms were full of small dry twigs and bracken, he returned to the cottage.

"Excellent!" Griswold declared as he took the kindling from Wat's arms. He placed it in the hearth, then handed Wat the fish. "Here. Clean these, and then we will have supper. Oh, and save the innards for the falcons. It's the best we can do for tonight."

Wat hated cleaning fish, but it was something he was familiar with and certainly easier than skinning a small mouse. When he was done, he carried the cleaned fish back to the cottage in one pail and the disgusting parts in another. He stopped at the door, surprised at how welcoming the place felt. The cleaning they had done that afternoon had greatly improved the cottage's appearance, and the fire crackled merrily, casting warm light throughout the dim room. It felt like he'd always imagined a home would feel.

"Thought you'd never finish." Griswold came and took the fish from Wat. "I'll roast these while you tend to your birds."

Wat hurried over to the makeshift nest and knelt beside his charges. "I'm going to have to come up with names for you." He held out a small piece of fish gut to the smaller one, who snatched it from Wat's fingers. Once the fish was in his mouth, the bird paused, puzzled at the strange taste. Wat laughed out loud. The falcon looked as if he would like to spit it out, if he could only figure out how. Wat held out a piece to the larger bird, who approached it with caution. She seemed less surprised by the taste, maybe because she took the time to smell the food first. The birds ate the fish, but not as eagerly as they had the mouse.

"Finicky little things, aren't they?" commented Griswold from behind Wat.

"You'd think they'd be so hungry they'd eat anything," Wat mused.

"You sound as if you say that from experience." Griswold's keen eyes searched Wat's face.

Wat shrugged. "What if I do?"

Griswold studied him a moment longer, then placed his hand on Wat's shoulder. "Come, boy. Let's eat."

As Wat sat on one of the benches, Griswold put the trout, still on its roasting stick, on the plate in front of him. He placed a piece of the boiled parsley root next to it. It smelled wonderful, and Wat's mouth watered. He reached for the fish. "Yee-ow!"

"Careful, it's hot," said Griswold dryly.

"Too bad you didn't care to tell me that sooner!" Wat said around his fingers, which he had stuffed into his mouth to cool.

"You didn't give me a chance!" said Griswold, laughing.

The rest of their supper passed without incident. They ate with quick efficiency in a companionable silence. Wat even ate the parsley root, which, when combined with bits of fish, wasn't too bad.

When Griswold was finished eating, he picked out a slender fish bone and used it to clean his teeth. He watched the fire, studying it intently, as if he saw images in the flames that Wat could not.

Trying not to stare at the old man, Wat looked over at the falcons. All during the meal, the birds had preened themselves, using their small, sharp beaks to comb and straighten their feathers. Now that they were groomed, they wasted no time falling sound asleep in their bucket, where they looked like two indistinguishable piles of fluff. Wat was tired, too, but doubted he could sleep that easily. His head was too full of questions.

"Might as well ask them, boy," Griswold said, startling him.

"Ask what?" said Wat, unwilling to admit anything.

"All those questions rolling around inside your head. Neither of us will get any sleep until you do. So, you get two questions and then we're off to sleep." Griswold leaned back and made himself comfortable.

How could the old man know what went on in his head? Wat wondered.

"I know what you're thinking because you're as transparent as a fine mist, boy. Every thought that enters your head flits across your face. That's question number one. You get just one more, so choose wisely."

"So it's not magic that tells you my thoughts?" asked Wat.

Griswold snorted. "Magic! That's just a word people use to explain that which they don't understand. Some people would call it magic that I can coax a trout to be my dinner."

"That's not magic!" exclaimed Wat. "I saw you do it, and I did it, too!"

Griswold's eyes glittered in the dim light. "Aye, boy. That you did. But now I have a question I'll throw to you. Does that mean it wasn't magic? Or does it just mean that you have the magic in you, too?" Chuckling to himself, Griswold rose and went over to the bed. Wat heard the rustling of the fresh leaves as the old man settled onto the mattress.

"Wait! What about my two questions?"

"You asked them, boy. And I answered."

"I only asked one. The first one you plucked out of my head, but I never asked it. That shouldn't count."

"Oh, all right. You have a point. You may have one more question," Griswold agreed.

Wat got down on the floor and settled himself as best he could in front of the fire. "Tell me of my mother," he said softly.

Griswold was silent a long time, and Wat feared he wouldn't answer. Finally he spoke, his voice low. "It was just she and I growing up. Her mother died giving birth to her, but she was a happy child, content to play among the wonders and creatures of the forest. As she grew older, she became lonely sometimes, but that was to be expected. Loneliness is part of life."

He shifted on the mattress, and Wat heard a soft rustle of dried leaves.

"I kept her safe, here in the forest. Safe from the raids along the coast, safe from the village oafs who would crush a maid with their brutal ways, but as she grew older, it ceased to be enough. And one night, one night she just didn't come home." The words carried the full weight of his grief, and he fell silent. He stayed silent so long that Wat wondered if that was all of the story he would hear. At last, his grandfather began talking again.

"When she returned the next day, she was light of foot and full of joy. In love, she told me. With a brave young knight who had asked her to be his. I worried as to how the villagers would accept a daughter of the forest. But none of my concerns mattered to her. A few days later she returned to the cottage, shattered, bitter. She packed up her things and left the next morning.

"I knew that he had somehow broken her heart. I had

warned her of that very thing all along. But I never guessed she was with child. If I had, I . . . well, I might have tried harder to bring her back here, where she belonged."

His grandfather grew quiet, lost in his memories.

Wat lay there in the heavy silence, his heart aching for his mother, feeling the pain in his grandfather's story. Unbidden thoughts rose to the surface. She had left the forest to find happiness, and he had run away to the forest to find the very same thing. He was glad it was dark so Griswold couldn't see his face and the confusion that plagued his aching head.

Griswold's voice called out through the darkness. "Don't fret on it over much, lad. You'll find there is much that seems senseless, but life will make it clear in the end. Dream well, and dream wisely."

chapter

· *9* ·

WAT TRIED TO MOVE HIS HEAD, BUT COULDN'T. SOME-
thing hard and unyielding encircled his hands. His neck
ached from being unable to move. His arms and shoulders
were numb from their forced position.

And thirsty. He was so thirsty. He opened his eyes. All
he could see was the ground at his feet and his long red hair.

But he didn't have long red hair. His was short and brown.

"Mother!" he cried out. He sat bolt upright in bed, his
body drenched in sweat, his heart thumping wildly. His
mother! She was the one who was trapped. Wat jumped
when a hand touched him. He heard Griswold's voice in his
ear, as if from far away.

"Wat, what is it? What have you seen?"

"It was a dream. But so real," Wat said.

"Tell me of your vision," his grandfather commanded.
He listened carefully as Wat told him of the nightmare that
had filled his sleep. When he was finished, Griswold said
nothing.

Realization dawned on Wat. "It wasn't a dream, was it?"

Griswold shook his head. "No, you have seen your mother."

Silence again. Finally, Wat spoke. "I must go to her."

"It will be dangerous. They still want you. And when they find you, they will do worse than what they have done to your mother. It may even be a trap," Griswold argued, but Wat sensed his approval.

"Aye. But at least they will have the right person." Wat stood up. The sun had just risen over the treetops. "I won't wait any longer. I'll leave now."

Griswold laid a restraining hand on his shoulder. "No. You must wait and leave here at dusk. You will have a better chance if you travel when it is neither day nor night, light nor dark."

"Why? Why can't I just leave now?"

Griswold leaned closer. "Because that's when the boundaries between this world and the other world are blurred. The spirits will be much closer then and can guide you."

Wat wasn't sure he wanted to be out when the spirit world was that much closer.

"It's when our magic is greatest," Griswold whispered. "Your powers and abilities will be strongest then."

Wat started to protest. "Powers? Abilities? How could I

possibly have a drop of power in me? No matter what I do, it comes out wrong. I tried to help the falcons, but now my mother suffers for my misdeed. I can do nothing without creating a mess. Perhaps I truly am devil's spawn, like they say."

"Never say that, Wat! Never!" Griswold's voice was terrible in his anger. "You have gifts that some of us can only guess at and that others will always be too blind to see. It is up to you to use those gifts wisely." His voice eased. "So far, you have used them only for good, no matter what the cost to yourself. That's not the mark of devil's spawn. That's the mark of a pure spirit."

Wat wasn't convinced, but he'd also learned it was pointless to argue. He changed the subject. "If I don't come back, will you . . . could you please take care of the birds for me?"

"Of course, of course. But have no fear. You will come back."

That was when Wat first realized that his grandfather could not read all of his thoughts. If he was truly able to do so, he would know that Wat was not planning to return. He would trade places with his mother. She would not be punished for *his* crimes.

"Come," Griswold said, rising to his feet. "We have much

to do today before you leave." He left the cottage, and as Wat often found himself doing, he followed.

They spent the morning setting snares. Griswold showed Wat how to do this using a bent twig and some long strips of grass. With luck, they would catch something to feed the falcons before nightfall. After they set the last of the snares, Griswold turned and began walking. Wat glanced up at the sky, anxious for dusk to appear. Three more hours, at least.

They walked for quite a while before Wat realized they weren't returning to the cottage.

"Where are we going?"

"Back to the oak tree where you found the young falcons."

"To the oak grove?" he repeated, trying to keep the fear out of his voice. "Won't they be looking for me there?"

"Aye. That they will," said his grandfather. "But not today. They have not entered the forest today."

"But how do you know . . ." Wat's words trailed off as Griswold turned and faced him with such a fiercely cocked eyebrow that his mouth snapped shut. In silence, he followed the old man. Soon the forest began to look familiar again, until, finally, Wat saw the giant oak in the distance.

When they reached the spot, Griswold paused, studying the grove intently. After a minute, he lowered himself to his knees and put his head near the ground. He turned his ear toward the earth, his eyes peering straight ahead as if he were looking down an invisible pathway.

"What are you looking for . . . at?" Wat asked. His voice came out in a small whisper.

"Elemental pathways, boy," his grandfather answered absentmindedly as he turned his head and peered off in another direction.

Wat gaped. Now he knew the old man was daft, just as his mother had claimed.

Griswold went on impatiently, as if he could sense Wat's doubt. "The pathways of the divine elements—earth, water, air, fire, and spirit. They run through the earth, crissing and crossing in an ancient pattern. It is their union with the earth that gives power." He pushed himself to his feet. "Well, they are intact, but they are somewhat fouled." He turned to Wat. "Sit. Over there." He pointed. "Out of the way."

Wat took himself to the spot Griswold had pointed to, and sat. Once again he looked to the sky, impatient to begin his journey back to the village. He opened his mouth to speak, but Griswold interrupted.

"Here is your first lesson. Our knowledge of things comes from the earth under our feet, the sky that hangs above our heads, the sweet water that burbles through the stream, and the very forest itself. The power resides in every living thing." Griswold looked up from counting his steps and gave Wat a sly look. "Even you. We walk and dance with nature, staying within the natural order of things to maintain the balance and preserve the patterns of life."

The old man had reached the far corner of the grove and, using his staff, cut a circle into the earth. He then drew two lines through it so they intersected in the middle. Then he pointed his staff due north from this mark and followed it until he came to the very edge of the grove in that direction. He carved another mark with his staff, the stick churning up rich, loamy dirt into four squiggly lines that reminded Wat of water running downstream. Satisfied, Griswold picked up his staff, again let it lead him to another point on the edge of the grove, and repeated this small ceremony twice more, drawing a circle with a dot at its center in one spot and a three-sided figure in another. He cut the last mark, a tight spiral, in the earth at the base of the oak tree, on top of the falcon's grave that Wat had dug. The carvings seemed heavy with power and mysterious meanings.

"Sacred sigils, boy. I have to restore the balance upset by man, and these symbols I cut in the earth reopen the doors to the elemental worlds which give this place its power," Griswold explained as he opened a pouch that hung from his cloak and took out a small handful of the contents. This he sprinkled over the marks in the earth. Feeling Wat's eyes on him, he turned. "The herbs needed for purification and cleansing," he explained. When he was done, he strode to the very center of the grove and raised his staff high into the air before thrusting it deeply into the ground in front of him. He threw back his head and began to chant. Wat couldn't make out the words, but they sounded strange to his ears, as if they were ancient and sacred.

Wat cocked his head, certain he could hear a faint humming, but was unable to locate it. He began to crawl over to the nearest mark to see if that was where the sound was coming from.

"Don't move!" Wat jumped back at Griswold's command, landing between two of the sigils. With a tingling shock, he felt a shimmer of energy leap from the sigil and run straight through his body until it reached the next sigil. That sigil began to hum and glow and sent an arc of energy onto the next, and the next, until the entire grove was boxed in by five radiant lines of power. It wasn't something Wat could see as much as he could sense it, hear it, feel it deep inside him. He felt like a moth pinned to a wall as the line of power ran through him. It didn't hurt, but it tingled, causing every fiber of his being to quiver.

Griswold stood in the center of the grove, clutching his staff, staring at Wat with his jaw agape. "By the gods . . ." Then he threw back his head and cackled with glee.

When the power had faded, Griswold pulled the staff out of the ground and lowered his arms to his sides. He looked drawn and gray, and Wat feared he would topple over. Instead, he leaned heavily on his staff, as if catching his breath. "I suspected you had some natural abilities, but never in my wildest vision . . ." His voice trailed off.

Wat stood, his knees a bit wobbly. "Wh-what was that?"

"Your power, boy. Your pure, untapped power." Griswold shook his head. "I've never seen any that strong before." He lifted his head and stared at Wat, as if truly seeing him for the first time. "Could it be . . . ?" he wondered aloud.

"Could what be? Are you all right?" Wat asked, concerned in spite of himself.

Griswold smiled. "I am fine. I am better than I've been in years," he said. "Thanks be to the gods." And indeed, he did look better, as if years had been lifted from his shoulders.

He turned and looked to the sky. "Dusk comes. You must go now."

"I should care for the birds before I leave."

"I will care for the birds. You must travel in the twilight. It is the most favorable time."

"But the birds—"

"Do not protest," Griswold ordered in a soft voice. "Remember, concealment will be your best defense. Do what you must, but keep safe." He gave Wat a little shove forward. "Use your power when you must, and put your whole heart and soul into it." He raised his staff in a gesture of farewell.

Wat turned and began on his journey. As he reached the thickening trees, he looked back over his shoulder. Griswold remained with his staff still raised in the air, the setting sun blazing red and orange all around him. His head was thrown back, his eyes were closed, and his lips were moving as if in a silent chant.

chapter

· 10 ·

WAT TROTTED THROUGH THE FOREST AS THE TWILIGHT deepened, turning the sky to deep purple. The worry over his mother urged him to hurry, and his fear and tiredness fell away. He still wondered how Griswold had managed to talk him into wasting a whole day before beginning his trip back to the village. He worried that something else, something worse, had befallen her since his dream.

The moon rose early, casting a pale, shimmering light on the forest floor. He did not trip or stumble once. As he ran, he planned his strategy, for he would need some clever thinking to get past the guards posted at the gatehouse.

The grounds in front of the large earthen mound on which the castle was built were kept clear of trees and shrubs and other hiding places. When Wat reached the edge of the trees, he circled around to the east side of the castle, keeping to the shadows. Once out of direct sight of the sentry, he crossed the open space to the edge of the moat and continued his approach, being careful to stay low.

He could make out the dark form of the guard at the gatehouse. It was tall and thin, which meant it was Denorf. Wat cursed his luck. He had been hoping to find the shorter, wider form of Ellis, who often ate too much at supper and slept through the first part of his watch. But Denorf was a sharp one, who took his duties to heart.

Wat would have a hard time getting across the bridge unseen.

He lay down on his belly, as close against the side of the bridge as possible, hoping that the meager shadow cast by the railing would offer him some cover. He crawled forward in an irregular pattern, moving, stopping, and moving again, in order to avoid detection. The hard wood bit painfully into his knees, but he ignored it. Sweat dripped down his face, but he couldn't lift a hand to wipe it for fear the gesture would call attention to himself.

When he drew close to the gate, he searched the bridge beneath his nose and found what he was looking for: a small stone lodged between the wooden planks. He picked it up and threw it back toward the bottom of the bridge. It thudded, making a small hollow sound on the wood before splashing into the water.

The guard stood up, straight and alert, peering into the darkness. He walk forward onto the bridge about fifteen paces. Wat pressed himself into the shadows, not even daring to breathe as the guard went to investigate. With the guard away from the gate post, there was just enough space for Wat to belly-crawl through the gate and into the outer bailey.

Once inside, past the guard, Wat laid his forehead on the ground and rested until his tense, knotted muscles finally stopped quivering. After catching his breath, he pushed himself to a standing position, wincing as a splinter from the bridge dug into his hand. Avoiding the path that cut through the center of the courtyard, he circled around the kitchen gardens.

The moon rode high in the sky now as Wat cautiously approached the inner courtyard. The village yards and shops, which would be bustling with activity come morning, were as still as graves. He passed the blacksmith shop and saw the flock of gray pigeons roosting for the night, their small heads tucked under their wings. He wasn't sure where he would find his mother, but he was certain she was here, somewhere within these walls.

Wat approached the center courtyard. Right before the second bridge that led to the lord's keep, he spied a large wooden structure. He had seen it only once before, so it took him a moment to recognize it.

It was the pillory. The large wooden trap they used to punish the villagers for their offenses against Lord Sherborne.

It was where they had held Will Thatcher until it was time to hang him. Even though that particular piece of justice had been carried out fortnights ago, Wat could still remember watching with fascinated terror as they placed Thatcher in the pillory. He had never dreamed a man could be punished so severely for wanting to feed his family.

Wat drew closer to the pillory and saw it wasn't empty. Even though he couldn't make out the face covered in matted red hair, he knew who was being punished.

·   ·   ·

HIS MOTHER STOOD, BENT FORWARD, HER NECK AND ARMS clasped in the large frame. Her eyes were closed, her face pale, her body unmoving. Wat fought down the fury that welled up inside him. He felt her shame as she must have felt it, pinned in the frame with all the villagers watching.

Calm. He needed to keep calm. He pushed the anger from his mind and forced himself to concentrate on the task at hand.

He wanted to run to her, but fear held him back. He drew closer with halting, clumsy steps, his misshapen foot managing to get in the way of his good one. As he approached, he could see the slight rise and fall of his mother's back as she breathed. She was, at least, alive.

His toe dislodged a broken cobble from the yard beneath his feet. The noise startled his mother out of her stupor. She looked up, and started as if she had seen a ghost.

Wat took a step closer. At his movement his mother opened her mouth as if to speak, but no sound came out.

"Mother?" he whispered.

"Is it really you, then?" she asked. Her voice, normally clear and sweet, croaked with disuse. "I thought perhaps you were a vision."

"No. I've come to help." He stood before her, uncertain what to do. His dream came back to him, the hair hanging in his face, the terrible ache in his neck and shoulders, and his dreadful thirst.

"I'll be right back," he said. He turned and ran to the village well. He took the common cup that was always there, filled it, and carried it back to his mother. He held it for her as she awkwardly tried to drink.

"Thank you, Wat."

He said nothing but gathered her hair up in his hands and twisted it into a long red rope and looped it around her neck, where it would be out of her way. He reached into the small space between the wooden prison and her neck and did his best to soothe her aching muscles.

"Ah, Wat," she said, closing her eyes as his hands worked the knots from her shoulders. "How did you know just what I needed?"

He shrugged, unwilling to tell her of his dream. When his hands grew tired, he sat down on the ground in front of her so they could see each other eye to eye. His mother studied his face.

"My heart is glad to see you, but you shouldn't have come. It is too great a risk."

"I had to," said Wat.

"But you shouldn't have. You're an outlaw now. With a price on your head." She raised her voice as much as she dared. "Do you know what Hugh will do to you when he catches you?"

Wat shook his head.

"Well, I do," she continued. "The whole village has talked of nothing else since yesterday. They will hang you for your crimes."

She paused and took a deep breath. Wat saw that she was trying to calm herself. "How have you managed to evade the search parties? Where have you been hiding?" His mother's eyes burned bright with her fear for him. "Never mind. Where you must go is the forest. If you travel deep enough within it, perhaps they will not find you. It is a big place, even they cannot know all of it."

"That's where I have been, Mother." Wat watched her closely, wanting to see her reaction to his next words. "I have found Grandfather."

Wat's mother closed her eyes, and her body sagged in relief. "He still lives." She opened her eyes, her voice urgent. "You must stay with him. He will guard you and keep you safe."

"He looks too old to guard a flea!"

"Do not mock him, Wat. He has powers beyond your understanding. They were most certainly beyond mine, when I was your age. But if I had just opened myself to the understanding of it . . . well, things would have been different. But I didn't, and now here we are."

"I can't leave you here like this," Wat insisted.

"You must. It will be better if you do so. They will release me at sundown today, and I will have been duly punished for my wayward son." A gentle smile crossed her face. For the first time, Wat realized that his mother was beautiful. "My wayward son with a true heart. That was a wondrous good thing you did, Wat."

Wat was surprised. He had not expected to hear those words. "You are not angry?"

"Nay. You followed your heart, righted a wrong, replaced cruelty with freedom. How could I be angry at that?"

"But . . . you are being punished for it."

"We are all punished in one way or another by these Normans. It is easier to bear when some good comes of it."

Her praise warmed him and gave him the courage to do what he knew he must do. "I don't want you to suffer anymore. I will stay and take their punishment."

"No!" she said forcefully. "You will do me no favors by staying. Do you think I will suffer less when they punish you?"

"But what will you do?"

She looked at the ground in front of Wat's feet. "Olin, the blacksmith, has offered to make me his wife, now that . . ."

"Now that I'm gone," Wat finished for her, hot shame suffusing him. What other fine things had his mother missed because of him?

"He is kind and gentle, if a bit superstitious," she said with a wry smile. An awkward silence stood between them. She studied him closely, as if memorizing his face. "You have been the most blessed thing in my life. All of the mistakes I've made are put right when I look at you." She sighed. "But now is the time for you to break free."

Wat could see the glint of tears in her eyes as she spoke. In the distance, a dog barked somewhere in the village. A voice called out for it to be quiet. His mother craned her neck around to look in the direction the voice had come from. "People will be up soon. You must leave before you are spotted."

"Shhh!" Wat hissed. Someone was coming.

The pillory stood out in the open courtyard. There was no good place to hide, so he stepped behind the large wooden frame and stood as close as possible, hoping his form would blend into that of the pillory. He emptied his mind of all thoughts and concentrated on being solid, rough-hewn wood.

"Who were you talking to?" The blacksmith's voice came through the night.

"No one." Wat heard his mother's voice quaver.

"Don't take me for a fool, Brenna! I heard you with my own ears!"

Wat heard a muffled step, then Olin spoke again. "Has Wat come back?"

There was a deep silence.

"Do you promise to help?" Brenna asked.

Wat heard Olin snort. "What help can I give against someone as powerful as Hugh?"

"It doesn't matter. Do you swear to help us and not turn him in?" Her voice was urgent.

Wat heard no reply but felt a presence in front of him. He opened his eyes, and the blacksmith jumped.

"How do you do that, boy!" Olin cried out. "How can you hide where there is no hiding place?"

Wat stared at the blacksmith, then shrugged. Would he keep their secret?

The blacksmith sighed. "Come out, I'll not turn you in. For Brenna's sake."

Wat and Olin walked around to the other side of the pillory, where Brenna could see them. "What can I do?" the blacksmith asked.

"Nothing for the moment," Brenna answered. "Stand over there, and when I call you, you must see that Wat gets back across the drawbridge before day breaks and people are about. He must get back to his grandfather, even if you have to carry him kicking and screaming."

Olin nodded and retreated a few paces. Wat's mother turned her gaze back to him.

"Will I see you again?" Wat's throat was so tight with emotion that he could hardly form the question.

"I will try to bring supplies to you and Griswold before winter sets in. If I can. But do not count on it. Now come; give me one last kiss."

Wat leaned up and gave her a kiss on her cheek. He could taste salt from her tears on his lips. He stepped back. "Good-bye," he whispered.

She waved at him as best she could with her hands shackled. "Now go." She smiled. "I can hear fortune's star calling to you, even if you can't."

Wat turned and, with his uneven gait, walked over to Olin. They eyed each other warily. Finally, the blacksmith spoke. "I'll strike up a conversation with Denorf. Ask him how his mail fits, if it pinches, the usual. Since I mended it for him less than a fortnight ago, the questions won't raise his suspicions. While we're talking, use that stealth of yours and get back across the drawbridge as quickly and quietly as you can. Got it?"

Wat continued to stare at Olin in silence, weighing his options.

"Well, must I carry you, boy?"

Wat eyed Olin's huge arms and grimaced. "No. I'll walk on my own."

The blacksmith grinned. "Smart lad," he murmured, before falling into step beside him.

chapter

· 11 ·

WAT ARRIVED BACK AT THE COTTAGE AROUND MIDMORN-
ing to find Griswold sitting on the front doorstep, waiting
for him. "About time you got here. Your birds were worried
about you." He creaked to a standing position and went
inside the cottage. Turning back over his shoulder, he called
out, "And they're hungry."

Wat followed the old man inside. He saw that Griswold
had placed the bucket near the hearth for warmth, and
the falcon chicks were peeping and flapping in a dreadful
uproar.

"They tried to talk me into feeding them this morning,
but I made them wait. 'Tis your job, not mine." Griswold
handed Wat a slab of raw meat. "They, however, were convinced they were near starvation."

Wat went and sat down on the floor by his charges. He
fished his knife out of his side pocket and began paring off
small pieces of meat for the frantic nestlings. He was glad
for something to do. He felt as if he had accomplished

nothing during the night. In spite of his fatigue, he was restless. As he settled to his task of feeding the birds, a sense of peace came over him. It was the same feeling he'd experienced the first night he had spent in the cottage.

He felt Griswold's eyes on his back, but he didn't mind. They felt kindly and concerned this morning.

The old man's voice spoke quietly from somewhere behind him. "You'll find that having someone, or something, to take care of always eases the pain." When Wat glanced up at him, he was staring out the window, his eyes seeing things far beyond Wat and the cottage. He heaved a sigh that, to Wat, seemed full of heartache.

He turned from the window and smiled. "They missed you, boy. Claimed the meat didn't taste as good from these old hands."

Wat smiled at the unlikelihood of that. "I can see how you've mistreated them."

Griswold reached out and flicked a nearby feather at him. Wat blew it away before it touched him. "Missed me."

"Of course." The old man sniffed. "I meant to miss."

Wat snorted. Then he jumped back as one of the falcons aimed for his finger instead of the meat. "Oh, no you don't!" Still looking at the birds, Wat asked Griswold, "Aren't you going to ask of my mother?"

Griswold turned his gaze back to the window.

"I learned a long while ago to have patience with regard to your mother," he answered at last. He turned back to Wat and smiled. "And I can tell from the look in your eye that Brenna will be well. Besides, knowing you, you won't be able to keep it to yourself much longer."

The birds had finished off the meat and seemed well satisfied. Wat wiped his hands on his tunic and picked up the larger one. The nestling looked puzzled, but didn't protest or try to get away.

"She was as I saw her in my dream," he said as he stroked the silky feathers. "Lord Sherborne had her put in the pillory to punish her for my thievery. She was glad to see me, but insisted I leave." He used one of his fingers to pet the small falcon and continued speaking flatly. "In the end, it was my moment of truth, and I failed to do what was right."

Griswold turned from the window and clucked his tongue. "Such self-pity in one so young!"

Wat looked up, startled at the censure in the old man's words.

Griswold leaned toward Wat. "That was no moment of truth, boy. That was a . . . a challenge, at best. And one you rose to, I might add."

"Where's the challenge in leaving my mother to pay for my sins?"

"Often letting someone help us is the hardest thing to do," Griswold replied. "Besides, a moment of truth is not a test, something to be failed or won. Nor is it earned. It is a simple moment in one's life when all the elements unite within to release one's true spirit."

Still sullen, Wat turned from his grandfather back to the falcons. "Anyway, she as much as said she would be better off without me. And she will be."

"Hmm." Griswold nodded his head. "Are these birds better off without their mother?"

Wat jerked his head around to look at Griswold again. "No! She died protecting them. Fighting for them."

"Exactly. Just as your mother fights for you. It is a different way from the falcons' mother, but do not doubt that she fights for you. And that it costs her much. No one is ever better off when parted from the ones they love."

A trickle of understanding began inside Wat's head. "And Olin?"

"Who?" Griswold's eyebrows drew up in puzzlement.

"The blacksmith. She said that he had asked her to marry him, now that I've . . . run off."

"Oh. Hmm." Griswold came over and put his hand on

Wat's head. "Well, with you gone, she will need someone, even if only a blacksmith, to look after. As I told you before, it eases the pain."

The full force of this new knowledge washed over Wat, cleansing him of the bitter taste of abandonment. Knowing her sacrifice, he felt more loved, yet more alone, than ever before.

To cover his grief and confusion, he turned his attention back to the falcons. He put the larger one back and picked up the smaller one. "We need to find names for you two."

"Have you named many things in this short life of yours, Wat?"

Wat looked up at where Griswold stood, looming over him. "No."

"Well, have a care! Names are not to be given lightly and must speak to the true nature of a thing." Griswold crossed over to the hearth. "Go outside and gather up a handful of dirt," he instructed. "If you are to name them, we must have a ceremony."

When Wat returned holding a handful of dirt, Griswold was kneeling by the hearth. He spotted Wat and straightened. "Bring the bucket of water closer to the birds."

Wat did as he was instructed, then knelt before the peregrines' makeshift nest. Griswold nodded. "Now pick one up and hold the bird in your hands, taking the full weight and measure of its true nature."

Once again, Wat reached out and picked up the larger of the young falcons. He held her in his two hands, feeling, judging, and closed his eyes. A vision of her proud, fiercely intelligent eyes filled his head, as well as a sense of patience and caution, as if this falcon would always weigh all the options and consequences before acting. "You are the more intelligent one. You are patient and wait to find out what is going on before you jump in. I will name you for that intelligence." The bird stilled, almost as if waiting to see what name would be bestowed. "Gaelen."

Griswold started slightly, but nodded his approval. "Good. Now touch your finger to the earth, then touch it again to the bird's head and say these words: 'May the spirit of the earth be like strength to you.'"

Staring into Gaelen's keen eyes, Wat solemnly repeated the words.

"Now dip your finger in the water there and place a drop on her head."

Wat did this and repeated the next set of words that Griswold gave him. "May the purity of this water cleanse your mind."

Griswold nodded again. "Hold out your hand."

Wat did as he was told and received a pinch of ash from the hearth. "Now sprinkle this along the bird's back and say, 'May the fierce beauty of fire fill your spirit.'"

Wat repeated the chant.

"Now lean close and blow gently in her face, but not too hard."

Wat took in a small breath, then exhaled it softly at Gaelen, who blinked and shook her head.

"May the air be strong beneath your wings and fill you with long life." The bird settled at these last words. "Now say, 'I name thee Gaelen.'"

"I name thee Gaelen."

When Griswold nodded his head toward the bucket, Wat put Gaelen back and picked up the smaller bird. Again, he held it in his hands and let his mind fill with the essence of the bird in front of him. Fierce, angry eyes filled his vision and a sense of impatience, eagerness. "You, however, are smaller and much too quick to stick your beak in before you are sure of the situation. And you are little and fiery, so I shall name you Keegan."

"Now repeat the ceremony," Griswold instructed in a quiet voice. Wat did, surprised at how easily he remembered the words. When he finished, he returned Keegan to the nest and rose to his feet, feeling calm and still inside.

From his place by the window, Griswold spoke. "How did you know those names?" he asked.

Wat shrugged and tried to remember where he'd heard them. "From stories Mother used to whisper in my ear, late at night, after the last of the fire had died down."

"She remembered, then. And told you of them." Griswold sighed deeply and closed his eyes, as if in relief, or thanks, Wat couldn't be sure. "It is more than I had hoped for."

When he opened them again, the moment had passed. "You have named them well," Griswold told him. "And remember, when you know the true name of a thing, it gives you power over it. Now come. I have something I want to show you."

chapter

· 12 ·

GRISWOLD STRUCK OUT ON A WINDING PATH THAT LED south, away from the part of the forest Wat was familiar with. Wat fell into step behind him, and they walked along in their customary silence. Wat let the sights and sounds of the forest soothe him, washing away his earlier sense of despair. He became absorbed in his surroundings: the tall regal trees, the filtered rays of sun, the small chipmunks and rabbits who scurried about on the ground. When he returned his attention to the path, he realized that he had no idea how long they had been walking. Nor was he sure he could find his way back without Griswold to guide him.

Griswold paused and opened his mouth to speak, but Wat interrupted.

"Yes, yes. I smell it. It's water again, but different water. A richer, wetter kind."

Wat smiled to himself, well pleased. Two could have at this sport.

Griswold eyed Wat. "Don't get cocky, boy."

In a short while, the trees grew larger than any Wat had yet seen. They were older, too. Their branches hung low, as if tired, but there was a deep underlying strength to them. Griswold stepped off the faint path they'd been following and headed for an especially dense tangle of trees. The old man wound his way through the trunks and disappeared. Hurrying slightly, Wat followed Griswold into the trees, then stopped, his breath struck from him.

Before him was a small pool, its surface a radiating mirror of gold and green light reflected back from the sun and branches above. The tiny body of water sat at the base of a slight hill, with a trickle of water feeding into it from above. Surrounding the pool were more of the huge trees Wat had noticed earlier. Some of their heavy, thick roots draped over the edge into the pool, as if they had reached down for a drink.

Wat turned to look at Griswold, who, in the strange reflective light thrown off by the water, seemed to have grown taller, straighter, younger. The old man was looking up at the surrounding trees, his face aglow.

"Here, Wat. This is where I come. This is the place from which I draw my strength." His voice dropped to a whisper. "This is the heart of the forest."

Wat believed it. He could feel the thrumming of the living trees all around him, like the heartbeat of a man, only deeper.

He followed Griswold to the edge of the pool, averting his gaze from his reflection. But again, some unspoken force called upon him to look. Slowly, he turned back to the pool, bracing himself for the impact of his own image.

He looked, then sucked in his breath. He was . . . beautiful. Well, not beautiful, exactly. But his eye. It was whole and unmarked. No scars, no ugly red stain.

"Come, drink with me." Griswold's voice interrupted his discovery. The old man reached into a small crack in the rock nearest him and pulled out an old, finely wrought silver cup. He dipped it into the pool, rippling Wat's reflection. The old man filled the cup with water, drank deeply, and handed it to Wat.

"Keep in mind, once you've drunk from the heart of the forest, nothing will ever be as it was. You will take part of the essence of the forest inside you, boy. And it will forever be a part of you."

Wat looked at the trees around him and tried to decide if he minded having the forest inside him. Having it be a part of him forever. Slowly, it dawned on him that he didn't mind. It didn't bother him a bit. In truth, it was a wondrous thing, to carry the essence of something as fine as the forest inside you, almost as if you were joined somehow, by some unseen force.

He looked up to find Griswold nodding at him. "Ever since my birth, I have been chosen as keeper of this forest, the guardian of this woods. It is my charge to tend to it, maintain its balance, clear it when fouled, and protect it when threatened. I have toiled for many years. But as you see, I grow old, my limbs are gnarled and stiff. Oh, I still have great power, but for how much longer?"

Griswold looked away from Wat and stared down into the pool. "There are so few left that follow the old ways. I have been greatly burdened by the fact that when I pass over, there will be no keeper for the woods."

Wat looked around him. "You mean it's your task to take care of all this?"

Griswold turned his gaze back to Wat and leaned forward, eager. "Until you . . ." he whispered. "The day I saw you, hope was born in my chest. And to find you were of my own blood!" He threw back his head and cackled with joy. "My wish, the one I hadn't even known I carried, had been granted. I have someone to pass all my knowledge to, my skill, my secrets." Griswold stopped smiling. "Providing the forest accepts you."

"Accepts me? How?" Wat asked.

Griswold shrugged. "We will begin teaching you her mysteries, letting you in on her secrets, but only she can decide if you are a worthy guardian."

"But what do I have to do to be worthy?"

"There is no easy answer to that," Griswold said. "But the forest will test you, take your measure, and if it likes what it sees, then you will have passed."

"Will it hurt?"

Griswold frowned. "What of pain? We are talking about a gift from the gods, a gift greater than most will ever dream of. What is a little pain when measured against such things?"

"You mean it *will* hurt."

"Ach. I mean no such thing. I only mean that it does not matter in the great scheme of things. Now, if you are willing, drink deeply and you will be set upon this new path."

Wat looked around at the clearing. Griswold offered him a chance to have a place in this world, to be a part of the great scheme of things here in the forest. Finally, he would belong somewhere, be needed by something, have a purpose to his life. There would be danger, especially with these Normans. And pain, if he correctly heard what Griswold was not saying. But his grandfather thought he could do it.

And, truth be told, Wat ached to do it. To become a part of this place, learn the same skills and secrets Griswold possessed. The idea thrilled him to his very toes.

Wat looked up and met Griswold's eyes. "I am willing," he said. He lifted the silver cup and drank the water, which was tinged gold with sunlight and sweeter than any he had ever tasted. As it ran down his throat, he felt his body begin to hum. The thrumming he had noticed became louder in his ears, and he could feel his own heart change its rhythm to match it. He felt the vibration of the earth where his feet touched it. The air shimmered and strobed; it, too, beating with the pulse.

Wat looked up to find Griswold peering at him intently. "What potion was in that water?" Wat asked as he handed the cup back to his grandfather.

Griswold threw back his head and laughed, a deeper, richer sound than Wat had yet heard from him. "Nothing, boy. Nothing but the purest of springwater mixed with the essence of the woods. Now come, it is growing late." He hoisted himself from the boulder on which he sat and waited for Wat to do the same. As they left the sheltered clearing, Wat noticed that for the first time, Griswold did not stride ahead. Together, side by side, they made their way back to the cottage.

chapter

· 13 ·

THE PEREGRINES GREW QUICKLY. WAT HAD BEEN WITH
Griswold for nearly a fortnight, and in that time the birds
had lost most of their fluffy, white down. They were now
covered in mottled brown feathers, with little bits of downy
fluff peeking out here and there.

"They'll be old enough to fledge in a week or so. Have
you given any thought to their first flight?" Griswold asked.
With a sigh he lifted Keegan from the table and plopped
him onto the floor.

"No, my thoughts hadn't gotten that far," admitted Wat.
But it was a good question. How would he get them to take
their first flight? He watched as Gaelen walked over—wad-
dled, actually—to see how Keegan was faring on the floor.
Together they went over to the hearth and inspected the
sooty ashes.

Wat knew the peregrines wouldn't stay with him forever.
They would need to make their own way in the wild. It
wouldn't be right to have these proud birds dependent on

him, any more than it would be to have them belong to Hugh, or Lord Sherborne. Wat knew the only thing that kept him from being just a kindlier version of Hugh was his intention to release them back into the wild. But thankfully, they were not ready to fly quite yet.

"Well, think about it!" snapped Griswold. "And get them out of my house!" The old man picked up the branch they used as a broom and herded the birds in Wat's direction. They had been busy testing their wings and flapping about in the ashes, and the hearth was a sooty mess. Wat stood up and gave a low whistle. "Gaelen, Keegan, come!"

Between the broom and Wat's voice, the young falcons' attention was diverted from the ashes. They followed Wat outside, their awkward bird gait matching his own uneven stride.

He sat down on a patch of grass with the sun on his back. The falcons sat next to him with their taloned feet stretched out in front of them. Wat smiled. They had no idea how silly they looked. He sighed, his feelings mixed at the thought of losing his companions. He had no idea how long they would stay with him once they learned to fly and hunt on their own. Their departure would leave a bleak hole in his heart, but then he would have more time to spend at the lessons Griswold set before him.

Ever since that day at the pool, Griswold had been busy stuffing knowledge into Wat's head: the names of plants and trees, their elemental properties and how to call their power from them, what their best uses were. It was endless. His grandfather had him listening to the stories the Ancient Ones told as the wind rustled through their leaves. Oak, birch, alder, and rowan all shared their stories with Wat until his head was so full it threatened to burst.

Griswold had taken him on treks deep into the forest, to hidden and forgotten nooks and crannies where the sacred places lurked. He'd instructed Wat on the sacred names used to invoke their power, although Wat had no idea what that power could do.

Today, Wat's task was to begin learning the sigils. As he sat outside with the falcons, he began tracing into the earth the elemental symbols that Griswold had been teaching him. In the ground next to him, he made a circle then crossed it with two lines. The rich earth rose up in furrows around his finger, and the rich loamy scent filled his head. Next, he practiced the sigil for air by drawing a circle and placing a dot in the center.

A light breeze rose on the air, and the nestlings twisted their necks and looked up to the sky. They had heard something that Wat had not. He looked up, alert.

A *kek, kek, kek* sounded overhead. A peregrine soared high above the trees. Gaelen and Keegan cocked their heads and watched, riveted by the acrobatics of the mature falcon. As Wat looked skyward, he wondered if the falcons recognized the bird as one of their own.

One of their own. The words touched on a familiar longing in Wat, and he was pleased to find it much less painful than before. While it was true that his mother loved him, she had been forced to leave his side and could not claim him as her own without causing herself much pain and suffering. He felt he had more in common with these birds in front of him than with any other person he had ever met, except, perhaps, Griswold. Wat sensed in the old man a love of the wild beauty and solitude of the forest that ran as deep as his own.

The peregrine in the air swooped down closer. He circled the small area where Wat, Keegan, and Gaelen sat, almost as if he were wondering what they were doing down there in the clearing.

"What are you doing here?" Griswold asked.

Wat jumped. As usual, he had not heard the old man approach. "I was just practicing the symbols you taught me."

Griswold nodded. "Good, good. I see that you have earth and air. Now show me the one for water."

Wat knelt down and carefully drew four squiggly lines in the dirt. No sooner had he finished the last of them than water rose up from deep below the ground and began filling the furrows he had made. Surprised, Wat looked up at Griswold. "Is it supposed to do that?"

Griswold stared in stunned silence as the sigil filled. "I don't know. I've never seen anything like that before." He looked from Wat to the sigil, then back to Wat again. "Your powers grow quickly," he said at last. "Hopefully, they will be ready in time."

"In time for what?" Wat asked.

"For when they come looking for you."

chapter

· 14 ·

"IF YOU'RE HUNGRY, PLUCK IT YOURSELF!" WAT GRITTED out through clenched teeth while glaring at Keegan. The young falcon glared back. Neither of them budged.

Gaelen sat off to the side, watching the dead pigeon that lay at Wat's feet as if hoping it would somehow miraculously pluck itself.

Over the past few days, Wat had been thinking of ways to prepare the young birds for life in the wild. One thing had become quite clear to him: there would be no one to prepare dainty little strips of meat for them to eat. They needed to accustom themselves to dealing with prey as they would find it. Besides, plucking fat little birds was a task he hated. The small, weightless feathers always found their way into his hair and under his tunic, and they clung to his hands for hours.

His plan had been first to give the falcons the plucked pigeons he snared, letting them tear the meat off the carcass themselves. They had taken on that challenge eagerly.

Next, Wat had tried to give them the pigeon unplucked. But they balked, refusing to touch the pigeon or even attempt to remove its feathers on their own.

Yesterday he had given up and plucked it for them. But not today. He was not going to cave in today. Hunger was a great teacher, and they had to learn. Soon.

Gaelen began her pitiful peeping again, and Keegan joined in. Wat did his best to ignore them and go about his chores, but their noise got sorely on his nerves. "Now I know why mother birds are so anxious to stuff food into young beaks!" he fumed at them, his arms full of the kindling he was gathering.

He ignored the falcons as long as he could. Finally, he could stand it no longer; his ears felt as if they would burst from the high-pitched clamor. Tossing aside the kindling, he stormed over to them.

"You want it plucked? So be it. I'll pluck it for you." He grabbed the dead bird from the ground and took it to the stump he used for a plucking post. He tore the feathers from the dead pigeon in a flurry of frustration. When it was plucked clean, he went over and waved it in front of Keegan and Gaelen's beaks. At the smell and sight of fresh meat that they could recognize, they became frantic with hunger.

"Oh, now you want it, do you? We'll see about that." He picked Keegan up with his free hand and carried him across the clearing. He found a branch that was within his reach and placed the bird on it. "There."

He went and fetched Gaelen and put her next to her brother in the tree.

"Now." He waved the plucked pigeon in front of them again. "If you want this, you're going to have to come get it. I will teach you something today or one of us will die trying!"

Wat walked back to the plucking stump and climbed up onto it. He held the pigeon out for the birds to see and jiggled it invitingly. "Come on now," he coaxed. "Gaelen, Keegan, come."

The birds shifted on their feet, unsure. Gaelen lifted her wings and stretched them a bit. Then, without warning, she launched herself from the branch. She flew straight to Wat, talons stretched out in front of her, and snatched the prey on the first pass. She tumbled to an awkward landing, her tail feathers spread out and her wings askew.

"Good girl!" Wat shouted, and leaped up into the air.

Keegan was not to be outdone by his sister, who was already tearing into her meal. With a screech, he pushed himself off the branch, sailing across the clearing to Gae-len and stumbling to a halt next to her. He pushed his way to the pigeon, forcing her to make room for him.

"Good job, Keegan!" Wat crowed, dancing around the clearing. He had done it! He had forced them to fly. He had expected to feel sorrow when they flew, as it would signal that their departure was near. But to his surprise, he felt nothing but joy. They had learned to fly without a real fal-con to teach them.

Wat settled himself on the ground and watched them eat, his chest filled with pride at knowing he had not held them back.

Suddenly he felt a hand on his back, shoving him into the ground. He twisted his head to get his nose out of the dirt and saw Griswold standing above him, one foot on his back, holding him down. As Wat watched, his grandfather seemed to shrink into himself, growing more still. It was as it had been at the trout pond. Griswold began to meld with the things around him until Wat had to rub his eyes to make sure he was still there.

"Be still, boy," his grandfather whispered in a voice so soft it sounded like rustling leaves. "Someone's coming."

chapter

· 15 ·

JUST AS WAT FELT A LARGE BUBBLE OF PANIC RISE UP TO
choke him, Griswold relaxed and removed his foot from his
back.

"Come out, then. Come out. It is only you."

Wat sat up and looked around. He wondered if his
grandfather had gone completely mad, for he saw no one.
Just as he opened his mouth to speak, a small cloaked figure emerged from the trees. As it passed out of the shade,
the sunlight glinted red off its hair.

"Mother!" Wat rose to his feet and went toward her, stopping when he reached her, suddenly awkward.

Brenna put her hand out to Wat's cheek. "I told you I
would try to come. Hugh seems to have accepted that you
and the falcons are lost to him—"

"Or that's what the man wants you to think," Griswold's
voice interrupted her.

"—and while it is not yet winter, I needed to see how you
were faring."

Brenna reluctantly turned from Wat to face her father. Wat watched them eye each other and wondered how long it had been since they had last spoken. At last Brenna nodded. "Yes. That is what he is claiming. Only he can know if it's what he truly believes."

The old man's eyes locked with Brenna's, as if he were going to argue the point further. He shook himself. "Ah, girl. Come here and let me look at you so I can see if the years have been kind."

Brenna looked surprised, but obeyed her father's command and went to stand before him. Wat expected him to reach out and touch his only daughter, but he didn't. His eyes bored into her with a look more intimate than any touch.

Finally, as if unable to stand it any longer, Brenna threw herself into her father's arms. At first, he didn't seem to know quite what to do, then began patting her awkwardly on the back. "Ah, girl. It has been far too long." He cleared his throat. "Come, daughter. Show us what you have in your sack. I certainly hope it is something tastier than two young falcons!"

The old man stood aside and motioned for Brenna and Wat to enter the cottage. "Besides, I'm sure your son is hungry. He always is."

Wat almost bumped into his mother as she paused at the threshold of the cottage. She stood and stared. "It is just the same," she whispered to herself more than anyone.

"Go in, go in. Don't make me stand out here all day," Griswold said from behind them.

She went in to the table and laid the small sack on it. She took out two round, freshly baked loaves of bread, a small cheese, and a sack of oats. She looked up at Griswold. "I tried to bring you things you couldn't find on your own. I know 'tis not much."

The old man nodded but said nothing as he sat down on the bench. Wat sat down next to him and watched his mother move around the cottage with the ease of one who had lived there a long time. She started to sit down, but stopped herself. Standing back up, she pulled an ale skin from her cloak and held it up before her father, smiling shyly. "And I remembered your fondness for ale."

Griswold chortled in delight. "Do you know how long it has been since I have drunk ale?"

"I can only imagine." She motioned for Griswold and Wat to begin eating, but refused any food for herself. Wat glanced from his mother to his grandfather, scarcely able to believe they were of the same blood. His mother, with her red hair and brown eyes, was so firmly of this earth. His grandfather was thin and lacking in substance, his gray hair and eyes the color of smoke. Wat could sense the unspoken words between them, hanging in the air like a dense fog.

Wat cleared the bread from his throat. "How is tiny John Thatcher, Mother? Have you seen him?"

Brenna frowned. "He is well, if just barely. But his mother lost the babe she was carrying."

Wat marveled at the unfairness of it all. Fat, powerful lords like Sherborne hoarding the bounty of the forests while others starved and sickened. Wat believed Griswold when he claimed the forests belonged to no man. They were gifts of the earth, to be used by man as needed and with proper thanks. Wat felt the truth in those words at the very core of his being.

"So, tell me of this blacksmith," Griswold's voice interrupted the silence. Brenna blushed, and Wat squirmed with discomfort for his mother. He knew how it felt to have that penetrating gaze fixed upon one's soul.

"Well, he first made his interest known some years ago." Brenna spoke in a soft voice, her fingers breaking a piece of bread and shredding it into tiny pieces. "And even though I made myself clear in my lack of interest, he has stood by me as a friend all these years, offering me his support. He has even shown some kindness to Wat."

"That's true," Wat agreed around a mouthful of cheese, glad to have words filling the air. "He chased Ralph and his gang away that day they were chasing me with the meat hook."

Brenna winced at the memory as Griswold turned to look at Wat.

"Besides," Brenna continued, pushing past that painful subject, "the protection he can offer me won't hurt either." She looked up from the pile of breadcrumbs on the table and smiled weakly.

Griswold scoffed. "You still place trust in those humans from the village?"

Her eyes flashed and she raised her chin. "We are different, you and I. I have come to accept that, and now so must you. I need voices around me, the sound of laughter in my ears. I'm sorry, Father, but there is none of that here in the life you have chosen."

"There is all of that here, and more," he answered. "Can you not hear the laughter in the gurgling of the brook? What other voices do you need than those of the birds waking you every morning?"

Brenna sighed, reached out a hand, and laid it over her father's fist on the table. "We have had this argument before. I understand your love of these things much better now than I did when I was young. But it is still not the life for me. I am no more of the forest than you are of the village." She looked over at Wat. "My son, however, seems to take after you."

Wat held his breath, wondering if the argument would continue.

After a long moment, Griswold took his free hand and reached out to pat Brenna's. "You are right." He turned to look at Wat. "Have you shown your mother your birds yet? Although, how she could have missed them is beyond me." The old man stood and began clearing the crockery from the table.

Wat took his mother outside to where the birds were cleaning themselves after their last meal. He did not know what to say, how she would feel about these birds who had been, indirectly, the cause of her punishment and humiliation. He cleared his throat. "The smaller one is Keegan, the larger Gaelen."

Brenna knelt down next to their bucket. "They are very beautiful. You have taken good care of them." She reached up and touched the feathers in Wat's hair. "They were lucky you were in the woods that day." She turned her gaze back to the birds, and together they watched them in silence.

Wat glanced up and saw Griswold standing in the shadows, watching them. He came forward and laid a hand on both of their heads. "Come, daughter, you should return to the village while there is still light and it is safe for you to do so." The reluctance was clear in his voice.

Wat and Brenna stood up and followed Griswold to the path. He took his daughter's face between his hands. "Do not come again, Brenna. I do not think we will be here much longer."

Brenna nodded, but Wat looked up at his grandfather in surprise. The old man had said nothing to him about leaving.

Brenna threw her arms around Wat, kissed him on both cheeks, then turned and was gone.

Wat and Griswold stood together at the edge of the clearing, watching long after Brenna had disappeared. When Wat thought she must surely be halfway to the village, Griswold finally turned to enter the cottage. Suddenly his whole body stiffened, and he whipped his head around toward the trees, sensing something that Wat couldn't. He stood like a deer that has sniffed danger on the wind, alert, poised for flight. Wat hardly dared to breathe.

After what seemed an eternity, the old man turned back toward the cottage. He said nothing, gave no explanation, but Wat could see there was a great sadness in his eyes.

chapter

· 16 ·

"Breakfast," Griswold called over his shoulder.

Wat made his way to the table, where they broke their fast
on the last of the bread Brenna had brought with her last
night and some of the oats that Griswold had cooked up in
a small iron pot he'd hung over the fire. When they were finished, they spent a few minutes tidying the cottage before
Griswold said, "We must go now. And bring the birds this
time."

"Did you hear that?" Wat asked the birds. "You get to
come this time." Normally, his grandfather insisted they be
locked up.

As Wat left the clearing, he whistled low. "Come, Gaelen,
Keegan." The peregrines rose up in the air and headed
toward Griswold. Wat ran to catch up. When Wat was right
behind Griswold, his grandfather sniffed. He paused long
enough to turn and look Wat over. "Come to think of it, a
bath would do you no harm." He turned and continued on
his way.

Ever since Wat had drunk from the pool, he'd begun to see the forest with new eyes. Each tree looked more alive, each branch more precious, the sound of the burbling brook in the distance and the slight rustle of the breeze in the treetops more meaningful than ever before. It had always been a place of comfort for him, but now he was seeing its strength, the power that a place so full of rich growing things had to offer.

Wat was so lost in his thoughts that it took him a while to recognize the path as it wound among denser trees, ferns, and undergrowth. "We are going to the pool?" he asked, his voice falling to a whisper.

"Yes," Griswold answered curtly, but did not slow down.

The falcons used the journey to practice their newfound flying skills. They alternated between circling in the air above the trees or launching themselves from branch to branch. Wat stopped to watch Gaelen make a spectacular swoop. She looked like a falling stone and then pulled up at the last moment.

Griswold stopped abruptly, and Wat, intent on his observations, walked right into him. He braced himself for a scolding, but Griswold merely grabbed his arm to steady him and whispered, "Do you hear it, boy?"

Wat cocked his head. He heard many things and didn't know which one Griswold was referring to.

"Listen to the rustling of the leaves, Wat. The Ancient Ones are whispering to you." Wat held himself as still as he could, and listened. The wind in the tree branches moaned and rustled, sounding much like the rise and fall of voices.

"Do you hear?" Griswold asked, his own voice scarcely louder than that of the breeze.

As Wat listened, gooseflesh raised along his skin. It seemed to him that the leaves were whispering a warning.

"Hurry, we've not much time." Griswold's voice interrupted.

Wat began walking faster.

It wasn't until the cluster of ancient trees that surrounded the pool came into sight that Griswold spoke again.

"Call them in, boy. The birds can't fly here. The branches are too dense."

Wat put his wrists out at his sides and gave a low whistle. First Keegan came to a wrist, then Gaelen. When they entered the canopy of trees, Wat placed the birds on a rocky ledge near the pool, where they settled and turned their attention to the water.

The falcons watched with intense interest as Griswold

retrieved his cup from the ledge and filled it with water from the pool. He drank deeply and then handed the cup to Wat, who drained it. As if this was some unspoken signal, the birds fluttered down to the edge of the pool and began to bathe.

Wat looked over at Griswold, half afraid the birds might be in trouble.

His grandfather waved his hand in the air in dismissal. "It's fine. It's as much their pool as anyone's."

Wat watched the falcons as they splashed water over their wings and used their beaks to comb it through their fine feathers.

"You may get in, too, if you like."

Wat pulled his tunic over his head and waded into the pool. It was unlike any water he had ever felt before. It was warm and soft and seemed almost heavy, as if he were bathing in oil. He dove under the surface and opened his eye. The deep, golden green was so beautiful it made his throat ache. He heard the thrumming again, and in no time his heartbeat matched that of the forest around him. And it wasn't gentle this time. It was full of power, strength, like the strong, steady footsteps of an unimaginably tall giant, or the slamming of an enormous hammer on a blacksmith's anvil. The water called to him, beckoning him, urging him to stay and live in the great golden light forever. With a gasp, he pushed himself to the surface and took a great gulp of air.

Wat climbed out of the pool, shivering slightly even though the air was warm and soft. Lying down on his stomach, he watched the sun's sparkling rays play off the water's surface.

As he lay there, an awareness of the land crept into him, as if his very skin were soaking up the earth. His breathing deepened and his heartbeat slowed. He became conscious of the rocks and soil, of deep roots reaching far into the depths of the earth, and throughout it all, a slow, steady rhythm that felt as if it were the heartbeat of the land itself.

He was part of it now. Not just a visitor, but part of its very essence. As it was a part of his.

The light breeze stirring the air filled his body and passed through him, just as it would rustle through the branches of a tree. Then the awareness dropped away from him—as if some tie had been severed.

He glanced up at Griswold, who sat with his chin cupped in his hand, staring hard at the pool's surface. His feet dangled over the edge of the water. Had he felt it, too?

Wat cocked his head. He thought he heard—no, not heard really, but *felt* something.

A small ripple disturbed the pool's surface. At first, Wat assumed he had imagined it. But no, there it was again.

"They have entered the forest," Griswold announced in a soft voice that sent fear seeping into Wat's veins like icy water.

Wat sprang to his feet and walked over to where Griswold stared into the pool. For a brief flash, he had an image of thundering hooves, jingling harnesses, the shouts of men. And then it was gone.

Griswold spoke again. "I had hoped we'd have more time. Your powers aren't strong enough, yet." He turned and peered through the trees. "We must run, go deeper into the forest, until your strength grows. Then we can face them."

Wat reached for his tunic and pulled it over his head. He looked around him, at this sacred place. He could still feel the remnants of the forest's heartbeat inside him, guiding his own heart. Had he truly found this place only to be chased from it? After years of painful longing he finally had a place to call home, here in the forest he loved so well. Were the Normans to steal this part of his life as well?

No, he thought. They would not. He turned to Griswold and spoke. "I am ready now. I will not run."

"Nonsense!" The word exploded from Griswold's mouth, and Wat realized his grandfather was afraid. For him.

"You've barely mastered a few basic sigils and tree names. You have no knowledge of how to call the other powers to your aid."

"But you yourself said you had never seen such raw talent before. Surely that is of some account."

Griswold became so agitated he began pacing. "One taste of magic and you think you can take on all the Normans?"

"It won't just be me. I'll have help," said Wat.

"My powers are great, boy, but I'm not certain even they are up to this," Griswold confessed.

"Not just your power." Wat looked over at the pool. Deep inside he felt as if the forest had already accepted him as the next keeper of the forest. "But that of the forest as well."

He turned back to Griswold. "I will not run anymore. I am sick of running and cringing in the shadows." He clenched his fists. "I want to drive these men away. Keep them from ever returning."

Griswold drew his eyebrows together and studied Wat, almost as if he hadn't ever really seen him clearly before. "I don't know if that is possible."

"But it is possible to try." Wat met Griswold's gaze, and the older man seemed to realize Wat could not be turned from this course.

"Very well," he said with a sigh. "But let us at least get to your place of power first so we can make the preparations."

"My place of power? What is that?" asked Wat.

"The oak grove, where you made your vow to the falcons and your own powers first awakened," Griswold said as he began walking away from the pool.

"But wouldn't our powers be stronger here at the pool? In the heart of the forest?" Wat asked as he followed.

"No. We must never risk them getting close enough to foul this place. Besides, in battle you do not use your heart to wield your sword. You use your limbs. Now hurry!"

chapter

· 17 ·

GRISWOLD STRUCK OUT STRAIGHT THROUGH THE THICK-est part of the trees, in a direction that would lead them directly to the oak grove. From far off, they heard the blare of a hunting horn.

Wat turned around. "The falcons."

"Don't worry. Your birds will meet us there."

"But they don't know where we're going," Wat protested.

"They will be there."

Wat had to trust his grandfather on this. There was no time to go back for Gaelen and Keegan.

The horn blared again. Wat turned to see if he could determine how far away they were, but his grandfather urged him forward. "Don't stop!"

The next time the horn sounded, it was closer and joined by the sound of braying hounds.

"You must go on alone. And hurry," said Griswold. "You are out of time." There was a new urgency in his voice. "You have claimed this as your moment of truth; now go to it."

Fear, anger, and nerves were lodged in Wat's gut, like huge stones. The weight of them threatened to pull him down, but he did his best to push them aside. He ignored the dull ache in his bad foot and kept going.

One of the hunstmen's hounds broke through the under-brush off to their right, his teeth barred in a vicious snarl. Griswold gave Wat a hard shove that nearly sent him to his knees. "Go!"

Wat hesitated as the dog bounded toward them with his hackles raised.

"I will take care of the hound," shouted Griswold. "Now go!"

Wat could afford to wait no longer. He turned and broke into a run. When he dared to look back over his shoulder, he saw Griswold's staff swing high in the air just before it descended upon the hound's thick head.

Wat ran, cursing at his clumsiness as he tripped and stumbled. He heard a loud screech from above, and then an answering cry. His falcons! He risked a quick glance sky-ward, where Gaelen and Keegan were circling overhead, keeping him in sight. Griswold had been right; they had followed.

The giant oak came into sight, reaching high above the

neighboring trees, almost calling to him, beckoning to him with its branches. Hearing the whinny of a huntsman's mount in the near distance, Wat tried to quicken his pace, but found there was no speed left in him. The bitter taste of fear rose in his throat.

Expecting to feel a hand on his shoulder any minute, Wat fixed his gaze on the oak tree. He cleared all sounds and thoughts of pursuit from his mind and let himself see only the oak. He pictured how it would feel when he reached its shade. Imagined how the rough bark would feel under his fingers. His whole mind filled itself with the giant oak tree.

And then he was there.

As he tried to catch his breath, his mind scrambled, trying to remember every bit of magic and power Griswold had told him about in the last fortnight. Sigils, he thought. He would use the sigils and call up the power of this place. He'd had no training yet in searching out the elemental pathways, but perhaps there would still be some trace of the original marks Griswold had made. The positions of those marks were permanently etched in his brain after watching the power spring to life between them.

He went directly to the nearest spot and was relieved to find a faint circle barely visible in the earth. Quickly, he bent to retrace the circle and carefully placed a dot in the center, then moved on to the next location, where he traced the symbol for earth. As he stood, he heard horses draw nearer and his heartbeat stumbled. Not yet. He wasn't ready yet.

He quickened to the next mark, where he bent to redraw the four squiggly lines that invoked the power of water. Hope coursed through him as the marks filled up with water, proof of what Griswold had told him. His abilities *were* strong. As he moved on to make the next mark, his gaze searched the grove, heart sinking when he saw there was still no sign of Griswold. He had hoped he would be here by now. The huntsmen were close. He could hear the labored breathing of their lathered horses.

Wat bent to draw the three interconnecting lines to invoke the element of fire, gasping as the earth beneath his finger turned hot. He snatched his finger back just as Hugh and his men broke through the edge of the clearing and spotted him. Wat, not wanting to look as if he was cowering on the ground, slowly stood up.

"Your mother led us right to you. I suspected she might, if she thought it was safe," Hugh said.

Wat remembered Griswold, poised on the doorstep after his mother had left, his face full of sorrow.

"Surely, you did not think you could get away with such a theft?" Hugh's voice continued. "Plums are a minor matter, but falcons?"

Wat was surprised at the strength in his own voice. "They don't belong to you or Lord Sherborne. They belong here. In the forest."

Hugh flung himself from his mount and strode toward Wat. "You stupid fool! This whole forest belongs to his lordship. Every beast, every bird, every tree is his. Even those sorry souls like yourself who live here. You all belong to his lordship. And he values you less than the beasts, have no doubt."

The last sigil. Wat had to get in position to invoke the last element. He turned and scrambled over to the great oak.

Behind him, Hugh laughed. "It is useless to run, boy. You will never outrun me."

Wat let Hugh think him a coward and covered the last few steps to the giant oak until he stood on the graves of the dead falcons, the ones he had dug with his own hands and watered with his own tears. He looked back up at Hugh. "This place is not yours. Not Sherborne's. Leave now and swear not to return, and perhaps you will be spared."

"Spared?" Hugh roared, then threw back his head and

laughed again. "Spared? By the likes of you?" He took another step toward Wat, and a shrill cry sounded high above. Hugh looked up in time to see the two falcons dropping like stones out of the sky. They bore down on him with their talons outstretched. Hugh backed away, throwing up his arms to protect his face. The birds came in at breathtaking speed, flying straight for his head. Their strong wings beat against him, talons slashing at his flesh wherever they made contact.

"Call them off! Call them off or I'll have my men shoot them down!"

Wat raised one hand in the air. "Gaelen, Keegan. Down." The birds pulled back and circled Hugh once before alighting on a nearby limb of the oak tree. Their keen eyes never left the huntsmen.

"You have trained them well," Hugh said, not laughing anymore. "For that, your death will be swift and painless." With one eye on the falcons, Hugh took another step toward Wat.

Wat backed away and found himself up against the tree. He looked down and saw new grass growing where he had buried Gaelen and Keegan's parents. He had to draw the last symbol if he was to have any hope. He leaned over to the side and tried to draw the last mark while keeping his eyes on Hugh. But he couldn't reach. His arms weren't long enough, and he didn't dare take his eye off Hugh.

Wat heard a slight rustle behind the oak tree, and a whisper-soft voice drifted in his ear. "Do not look around, boy. But I am here. I am with you." Wat could feel Griswold's presence in his very bones. "Use your power, boy," Griswold urged, his voice still nothing but a whisper. "Remember the sigils. Use them. Use the lay lines. They are yours to command. Call upon everything you know and use it. Now. While there is still time."

A gust of breeze sent Wat's hair fluttering, and as he lifted a hand to push it out of his eyes, they landed on the feathers. The ones he had taken from the two dead falcons. Without thinking, he snatched them from his hair and reached down to the ground, where he used the quills to trace the last sigil, the spiral that represented the living spirit in all things.

Barely had he lifted the feathers from the earth than he felt the lines of power snap into place, surging from one mark to the next, filling the grove with a steady hum. The energy pressed against his skin, like a swell of floodwater after a harsh rain. Wat struggled for a moment, then stopped. He had called this power, and it had come. Now he must ride it out and hope for the best.

Wat gave himself over to the forces he had called. They throbbed under his feet, then he was rising up and up, the power washing through him, leaving the sensation of racing through the air, head thrown back, and arms outstretched.

chapter

· 18 ·

As the power sprang to life, Gaelen and Keegan rose up in the tree again, screeching and calling out, circling the clearing. The other falcons, the tame falcons on the wrists of the hunting party, shrieked back in response. They grew agitated and unsettled, straining against the wrists that held them. Keegan and Gaelen continued circling the grove, calling out to the captive falcons, as if trying to work them into a frenzy. One by one, they rose up, fighting and straining at their leashes, trying to join the falcons in the air.

"'Tis the work of the devil!" cried one of the bowmen. He fell to his knees and raised his fingers in the sign to ward off evil.

Hugh ignored his panicked men and advanced slowly, savoring the moment like a victorious cat with a particularly elusive mouse. His eyes narrowed and he pulled his knife from its sheath. "Enough of this game, boy. Your time has come."

Wat cried out as a sharp pain pierced his sightless eye. At

first, he thought it was Hugh's knife. But when he opened his good eye, he saw that Hugh still held the knife in his hand.

The pain grew worse before Wat realized what was causing it.

Light.

For the first time ever, he could see light with his bad eye. For an eye born into darkness, so much bright light was excruciating. He closed his eye and covered it with his hand, but still the light crept in, a hot, searing pink as it poured through his fingertips. Try as he might, he was unable to keep the light from flooding his eye.

Squinting as hard as he could, Wat pulled his hands away from his face. The light on his eyelids burned like a fire-red brand. Slowly he opened both his eyes.

He forgot about Hugh and his knife. He forgot everything when he realized . . . he could see.

And so well! With his good eye he could see not just the bowmen and Hugh but far back into the trees and beyond. When he looked at the eyes of the mounted horsemen, his vision was so sharp, he could count their eyelashes. And his bad eye! No longer was there just darkness. He could see light and shadows, shapes and movement.

Suddenly Wat cried out and jerked back against the tree.

His lame foot began to cramp. It felt as if his toes were being ripped from his foot, forced to uncurl and stretch out. His toenails prickled and stretched, as if they were being pulled from his toes. He tottered on one foot, his twisted one no longer able to help support his weight.

A tingling sensation traveled down from his eye through the rest of his body. It was as if tiny flower buds, or leaves, were sprouting and unfurling all over him. He could feel a *pop, pop, pop* as something burst out all over his skin. Wat saw a look of horror cross Hugh's face. The man took a step backward, his knife dangling forgotten in his hand. Wat turned to look down at his arms, wanting to see what had horrified the seasoned hunter. He gasped. Where his arms had been were two large wings covered in brown-and-white feathers.

Too many things were happening all at once. He couldn't grasp them all. The sensations made his head ache and pound. He was spinning inside his head, faster and faster. He would have screamed if he could. But when he opened his mouth, the scream turned into a screech.

"*Keeeek—keeeek!*" he cried.

He opened his mouth to speak again. "*Keeeek.*"

From above, Gaelen and Keegan answered his cry with their own. From their places on the huntsmen's arms, the captive falcons screeched back in answer. Almost as one, they surged up from the wrists that held them, the powerful muscles of their wings straining against the leather ties that kept them prisoners. With a small *snap*, one bird burst free, shooting from the huntsman's arm like a stone from a catapult. *Snap, snap, snap.* All around the clearing, the birds broke free from the leather ties that held them down. They soared into the sky, up to where Gaelan and Keegan circled.

Hugh unstrapped the huge bow from his back and fumbled for an arrow from the quiver on his shoulder.

Wat looked up at Hugh, who seemed to have grown larger and loomed above him. He reached out, beseeching Hugh not to shoot. The sudden movement caused the wind to rustle through his wings and carry him forward.

The urge to stretch those wings was so overpowering he couldn't ignore it. He spread his arms wide, as wide as they could go, wanting—no, *needing*—to rise up into the air. Not even aware of how he did it, Wat raised his wings, pushed off, and launched himself into flight.

As he pumped his newly formed wings, the muscles of his back rippled at their movement. He thrilled at the powerful feel of them as they moved through the air. Air that felt like water as he worked his wings against its currents.

The wind rushed in his face, and he could feel it moving through his feathers.

Higher and higher he rose, his first flight carrying him high above the oak grove. He climbed up into the sky, where Gaelen, Keegan, and the others seemed to be waiting for him.

Why? he wondered. Why would they be waiting for him?

Swiftly, the memories rushed at him. Intruders. A threat to their home. He circled the grove and all the falcons seemed to fall into place behind. As he looked down he could see the huntsmen, as small as beetles, in scrambling disarray. But that wasn't enough. They needed to be chased from this place. Driven from the forest. Convinced never to return.

Wat angled his wings and launched himself downward, plummeting to the ground like a falling stone and heading straight for Hugh. Behind him, the other falcons followed, streaming out of the sky like spears from the heavens. One of the men looked skyward and gave a shout. One by one the huntsmen froze as a fury of falcons descended upon them with their talons raised.

Faster than the men could blink, Wat and the falcons were on them. As Hugh looked up, he threw his arms up to cover his face, but he was no match for Wat's fury. He slashed at Hugh's head with his talons, flapping his wings, lunging and striking, ripping and slashing.

Hugh threw himself down on the ground, rolling onto his stomach, and covered his head with his hands. And still Wat attacked.

All throughout the clearing it was the same. Wings beating against their heads, talons raised to their faces, and sharp beaks lunging for their defenseless eyes, the huntsmen tried to fend the falcons off long enough to reach their horses.

A lucky few succeeded. The rest, realizing there was no escape, fell to their knees, calling for help.

Slowly, the falcons began to tire, their fury evaporating as the men were driven back. A few of the huntsmen managed to crawl to their horses, and as the falcons finally withdrew their attack, others tried to do the same.

Wat pulled back from Hugh's still form, and rose up higher in the sky to watch as the men struggled to find their way to safety. Calmer now, he caught a strong breeze and rode it, letting the wind cleanse him, soothe him. He circled the clearing and saw that nearly all the men had left; even Hugh was being helped onto his horse by one of the other huntsmen.

Wat circled the clearing twice, enthralled with the gentle *swoosh* the air made in his feathers. He longed to rise up into the sky, even higher, and soar, but something called him downward. As he drew closer to the ground, he grew nervous, panicked almost. He wanted to soar back up into the sky, up into freedom and safety. But he couldn't. The nameless something called him downward.

Downward he went, faster and faster, the ground rushing up at him until, suddenly, there was nothing but blackness.

LIKE A TRICKLE OF WATER FILLING A POOL, WAT FELT himself begin to return to his body. It felt as if the very essence of himself had been scattered to the four winds and was only now journeying back.

Slowly, he opened his eyes. He was lying at the base of the oak tree. Disappointment flooded him when he realized he could only see out of his one good eye, the images no sharper or far-reaching than they had ever been.

"Oh, thank the gods," Griswold whispered from where he knelt beside Wat.

"Wh-what happened? Are they gone?" Wat asked.

"Yes. Yes, they are gone. And I've never seen such an undisciplined, chaotic, slapdash bit of magic in my life," Griswold said, scowling furiously at Wat.

"But it worked, didn't it?" Wat asked, trying to sit up.

Reluctantly, Griswold began to chuckle. "Yes, boy. It did. No villager or huntsman will come near this place. Not in their lifetime anyway."

An indescribable feeling welled up in Wat. He could hardly believe it. It had worked. Somehow between his power and that of the forest, they had managed to drive the intruders away. Hopefully never to return. And if they did, Wat would chase them away again. He would spend his whole life chasing such men as these away, if need be. They might control all of Britain, but they would never control these woods. Or him.

A question hammered at the back of his skull, but he was afraid to ask. Afraid that perhaps he'd dreamed the whole thing. "Did I . . . did I really . . ."

Griswold raised a shaggy eyebrow. "Hmmph. Indeed you did," he said, nodding his head toward Wat's arm.

Wat looked down and saw a dozen small pinfeathers, fluttering gently in the soft breeze, sticking out of his wrist. Awestruck, he reached out with his other hand and plucked one. It tugged at his skin, until, with a little jab of pain, it released. He glanced up at Griswold. "It *is* true," he whispered, filled with wonderment.

"Of course it is," muttered Griswold.

Still holding the pinfeather in his hand, Wat scrambled to his feet. "Are you able to do that? Is it something I'll be able to do it again? Was it the sigils? Or the falcon's grave I was standing on?"

"Silence," Griswold said, holding up his hand. "You have managed a very great thing today, Wat, but make no mistake. Your training has only just begun. You will understand the true depth of your power and abilities with time."

Wat opened his mouth to ask another question, but the words died on his tongue as his gaze settled on the treetops. All the escaped falcons sat in the branches, as if waiting for him. Nearly a dozen assorted kestrels, merlins, goshawks, and peregrines roosted in the trees. But where were Gaelen and Keegan?

As if his very thoughts had called them, Gaelen and Keegan appeared overhead, circling once and then alighting on one of the branches in the oak tree.

"Well," Griswold said, "I have much work to do here in order to purify the grove. While I am busy, go ahead and tend to your birds."

As Griswold began the purification ceremony, Wat went over to the nearest tree and called the falcons to him. Much to his surprise, they came, meek as newborn kittens. One by one, they settled in front of him. Wat greeted each bird in turn, praising them for their bravery and stroking the glossy feathers along their backs. He patiently untied the little bells from each of their legs and tossed them aside.

Then he removed the leather leashes that had gotten tangled around their talons, and released the falcons back into the sky.

And as he watched, his heart soared with them.